A Trinity Heart Novel
Book One

Trinity Heart
Snow Angel

JULIE BRAGONIER MINNICK

Cover art ©2014 by Julie Bragonier Minnick
Cover Model: Allison Minnick
ISBN-10: 0-692-26370-5
ISBN-13: 978-0-692-26370-9

Dedication

This book is for Melissa,
who found her Life Path.

Chapter One

Trinity lay in shock: cold, bleeding in the snow. Her twin brother cradled her head in his lap, crying. The demon Roan had sunk his animal fangs into her side, ripping her flesh away. She was dying; her grisly premonition was coming true.

While Trinity's blood stained the snow red, Roan and the other demons fought against her angelic friends. If someone had warned her months ago that this is where her life would end, she would not have believed them. Vampires and Werewolves would have been easier mentally digested than the ethereal horror and glory she was witnessing. As she bled out, her wound gaping, her mind wandered back to the beginning.

....

Mid-November, the first snow had yet to fall. Trinity Heart, a junior at Shadowland Academy stared out the window of the commons room. Shadowland was an elite boarding school that lay hidden in the countryside of England. Dusk had fallen, twilight was near, and the air was dark and mysterious. A light fog covered the school grounds; hovering over the grass and making the setting feel...

"...devious," she whispered.

The moonlight shined down on Trinity creating quite a delicious sight. The way the moon lit her creamy white skin, black hair and sparkling blue eyes was picturesque. Her cherry red lips contrasted with the monochromatic portrait.

"Full moon tonight," said Nicholas, Trinity's twin brother.

He leaned in the doorway watching his sister. She glanced at him over her shoulder and turned her attention back to the sallow shadows the moon cast over the landscape.

Nicholas was every bit Trinity's twin. He too had midnight hair, pale skin and blue eyes. People often commented that he looked made-up like a doll, but Nicholas hadn't worn make-up a day in his life. Their appearance was not the only thing the twins shared. They had an uncanny connection the way many twins do. They could feel each other, know what the other was going to say, and even predict the other's next move.

"They're out there," Trinity whispered. "I can feel it."

Nicholas walked silently over to his sister and searched out the grounds through the window pane. The glow from the full moon lit the gothic architecture of the buildings, each dark shadow enhancing the drama.

"Something bad is…" Trinity started.

"I know," her brother finished.

They waited in silence. Watching.

"Ever since they came, nothing's been right," Trinity said, her breath fogged up the window.

"They destroy everything they touch," said Nicholas.

"Including Cole Hopkins," Trinity added, sadly.

"They've only been here since September and yet their darkness has permeated everything," Nicholas said.

"Cole used to be such a good kid. We've known him since grade school," said Trinity. "And now the Dark Ones are changing him," she added, referring to the newly-enrolled students at Shadowland Academy.

Cole Hopkins was from San Diego, California. He had sandy blonde hair, blue eyes and just enough freckles to make him look like the surfer that he really was. He was Captain of the Rugby team, received good grades and was genuinely a nice guy. Last year he was voted in the year book as, "sophomore with the most potential to change the world." Everyone liked and respected Cole.

This past summer, out of the blue, his parents divorced and it hit Cole hard. While he still maintained his Captain status on the rugby team, his grades had taken a dive this semester. Trinity talked with him at the beginning of the school year about his family. He was hurt, but coping.

Then the Dark Ones sank their talons into him and his entire demeanor changed: dark, bitter, cruelly confident.

Trinity and Nicholas named the new foursome the "Dark Ones". The twins sensed something just wasn't right about them. They all had evil, empty eyes that pierced through you.

Zoenn, the leader of the four, had raven hair to match his beady eyes. He was controlling and cruel. Roan, the Dark One that had taken a vile interest in Trinity, had brown hair and a wickedly mischievous grin that curled to one side. Marquis had blonde, almost white hair. He always seemed solemn and emotionless. Ivory, the only girl among them also had short black hair, but she had yellow-green eyes that reminded Trinity of a lizard. And what really freaked her out was Ivy's forked tongue.

The four troublemakers strode around campus in black trench coats with an air of purpose. They were inseparable, and lately Cole Hopkins had become an addition to their clique. He had not become one of them, but they had embraced him, and were nurturing and molding him into something cold. Once in a while Trinity saw a glimpse of the real Cole, the kind, cheery kid he had once been. Maybe there was still hope for him.

No one had been able to pin the odd and freaky things that had been happening around campus on the four Dark Ones, but Trinity and Nicholas knew they were the culprits. Tonight would be no different.

"We have an exam in the morning," Nicholas said.

"I'm dreading the outcome tomorrow," Trinity said in a hushed voice.

"More than your test?" Nicholas said, with a wry grin.

Trinity returned the smirk, which slowly dropped into a worried frown.

"There's nothing we can do," whispered Nicholas.

Trinity looked up at her brother and pursed her lips. Nicholas was right, there was nothing she could do and she needed to rest.

Chapter Two

Trinity awoke, startled. She slammed straight up in her bed with a cold sweat. It was morning and, as Trinity had predicted, something was wrong.

She whipped back her covers and slipped on her pleated, black and white plaid skirt. She had added a couple chains draping from belt loop to belt loop. She grabbed her combat boots and pulled them on over her striped thigh-high socks. She did not bother brushing her unruly hair that flowed down her back. Something was amiss and she needed to know what.

As she ran out of her room, she nearly collided with her brother who was also dressed and anxious.

"What?" Trinity asked, knowing he had news.

"Ophelia woke up this morning chanting nonsense," Nicholas informed her.

Trinity and Nicholas hastily made their way to the infirmary to see Ophelia. They ran across the icy yard in the pale morning light. They slowed their pace as they entered the small hospice at the school.

Ophelia was sitting on one of the cots in her cotton nightgown, feet planted squarely on the ground, rocking and humming gobbledygook. Trinity looked around, the Headmaster and two nurses were discussing things in the office. Nicholas sat next to Ophelia and placed a hand on her shoulder.

"What have they done to you?" he whispered.

A small grin slid up Ophelia's face as she continued babbling quietly. Her grin slipped away. Her eyes were focused off in the distance.

"Can you hear me, Ophelia?" Trinity asked.

No response. Ophelia simply continued murmuring nothings.

Trinity leaned in to listen.

"Some obscure language," Nicholas whispered.

"Nothing I recognize," said Trinity.

Nicholas knew it was no use trying to talk to Ophelia. She was in a trance of some sort, chanting a language neither of the multi-lingual twins recognized. They looked at each other and knew the Dark Ones had done this.

"Why?" Trinity asked, baffled.

Her brother simply shrugged his shoulders and shook his head. The two of them slipped out of the infirmary before the

Headmaster and nurses came back to check on Ophelia. They walked back to their dorm in silence. The only noise was the miniature cracks in the frosty ground as it crushed beneath their boots.

Nicholas looked disheveled. He had thrown his black wool coat over his half buttoned and untucked shirt. His tie hung loose around his neck. Even with his raven hair tousled and unkempt he was remarkably striking and handsome.

Trinity took her brother's hand beneath their woolen sleeves. He gave her a small squeeze. Her black nail polish stood out against her pallid hands. Without a word spoken, they understood each other's nervousness. There was a lingering heaviness and only the two of them seemed to notice.

Nicholas put his arm around his sister's shoulders. Trinity's pale skin, long black hair, coupled with her lovely features, stark blue eyes and crimson lips, made her looking like a walking painting. The twins looked at one another and without a word spoken they both knew they needed to find a way to stop the disturbing happenings.

Chapter Three

Trinity walked down the hall to her second class, the majority of her books in a messenger bag slung over her shoulder, but she carried a few that did not fit. She was deep in thought and did not even see Sabrina, the most popular girl in school, walking toward her with her little groupies. Marquis, the almost albino Dark One, had his arm draped over Sabrina's shoulder, with Roan in tow.

Sabrina slammed into Trinity, causing her books to fly. A cruel laugh escaped her full pink lips. Sabrina's cult followers did as she did, and giggled. She and Marquis kept walking down the hall, occasionally looking back at Trinity kneeling on the ground gathering her books. Marquis' face was cold and hard, expressionless.

Roan hung back and with one swift movement was by Trinity's side.

"Hey beautiful," he crooned malevolently as he placed one hand on her thigh and handed her one of the books off the ground with the other.

Trinity jerked up brushing Roan's hand from its inappropriate resting place. His smirk curled up on the left side of his face. She curtly turned and walked away.

This was not the first time Roan had made unwanted advances. Trinity shuddered at the idea of Roan's hands on skin. As for Sabrina, Trinity could deal with means girls. It all stemmed from Sabrina's resentment of Nicholas.

Last year, Sabrina and Nicholas had dated for almost the entire year. The week of finals, Nicholas found out that Sabrina had been cheating, copying off all his papers. When he confronted her, she denied it and insisted on her innocence. Nicholas had no choice but to break off their relationship and report her to the Headmaster, otherwise he would be expelled. Sabrina was sent home for the rest of her sophomore year. She came back her junior year under protest. She had wanted to transfer to Scarlett Cross Boarding School in France, to avoid the embarrassment. But Scarlet Cross would not accept a previously-expelled student. So, under duress, she was sent back to Shadowland Academy, where she came back with a vengeance and pure hatred for Nicholas and Trinity.

Sabrina, blonde and beautify, was a magnet to kids of all sorts. Each of whom would do anything to be considered a part of Sabrina's crowd. So Sabrina spread little lies about Nicholas and

Trinity to turn the other students against them. Most of the students knew the lies were not true, but they did not want to confront Sabrina lest they become the object of her ridicule.

Trinity did not care what Sabrina said about her. When Sabrina was not around, all the other students talked bad about her. It was a twisted little game they all played.

"Trinity," Riley called, trying to break Trinity's thoughtful trance.

No response.

"Trinity," Riley called again.

No response.

Riley smacked the back of Trinity's head with a notebook.

"Trinity!"

She snapped out of her daze.

"What was that for?" Trinity said with a wince and a smile, rubbing the back of her head.

Riley was one of Trinity and Nicholas' closest friends. They had been together since third grade, and yet Riley did not understand Trinity at all. Riley was completely enamored by the Dark Ones. She thought they were murky and mysterious. Riley was incapable of taking anything seriously and did not understand that there truly was pure evil in this world. She thought anything wicked was simply Disney-style Hocus Pocus. Riley was pure goodness in and out and incapable of comprehending evil. Riley thought it exciting that Roan had taken an intense interest in Trinity. But Trinity felt hunted by a hungry predator.

Trinity and Riley headed off to World History together as Riley chatted about Anthony, her secret crush. Anthony had become a part of the little friendship ring their freshman year. But Anthony had a secret crush on Trinity, which was not too much of a secret. Trinity pretended not to notice and constantly encouraged Anthony to take an interest in Riley.

After class, Trinity snuck away from Riley and met her brother outside the infirmary, as if it was planned. The twins knew what each other was thinking. Uncanny how twin telepathy works.

The hospice was empty. The twins exchanged confused looks. They quietly looked in each of the rooms. The door to the room at the very end of the hallway was closed, with a padlock on the outside of the door. Trinity and Nicholas snuck quietly down to the room and peered inside the skinny window. Ophelia was locked inside the padded room. She was thrashing about and grunting. The twins stared, disbelieving. This morning she had quietly been chanting in a foreign tongue and within hours she had become an animal trapped in a cage.

Suddenly Ophelia's body thrashed against the door, the right side of her face smashed up against the window, her eyes wild and possessed. A blood curling scream pierced through the window. She was a girl in pain, not in control of her own body. Her eyes bulged, her hair was matted and her body soaked in sweat. When she whipped away from the window, she fell to the floor, her fingers curled as a bird of prey. Her white cotton nightgown was torn and the twins could see freshly-healed slash marks across her back. Trinity pressed her face close to the window to have a better

12

look. She thought that the wounds had probably been inflicted last night. Each wound was barely closed over, still red and swollen.

Whatever the Dark Ones did last night, Ophelia had been their victim.

"What can we do?" Trinity asked her brother already knowing the answer.

"If we ask too many questions we could become just like her," Nicholas warned.

Trinity scoffed, angry.

"I'd like to see them try."

She looked back at Ophelia rolling on the ground moaning, holding her stomach.

Ophelia's mouth opened wide as if she was going to scream and yet a small voice came out. It was Ophelia's real voice.

"Help me," she eked, wide-mouthed, without moving her lips. Nicholas stared amazed at the phenomenon. It was as if Ophelia was a host to an unseen force. Then out of the same wide opened mouth came a horrendous, animalistic voice yelling in the same ancient language the twins heard Ophelia use earlier.

Suddenly Ophelia snapped to the bed, sitting on the edge, feet planted squarely on the ground rocking back and forth, chanting in a child-like sing-song voice. Trinity sucked her breath in because she recognized what Ophelia was saying.

"Ring around the rosy, pocket full of posies, ashes, ashes, we all fall down...all because of me." She repeated her rhyme incessantly as her nail carved a circular ring on the top of her hand until her skin tore.

13

"We are going to have to move her to General Psychiatric Ward in London," came the doctor's voice from down the hall.

"Her parents will be meeting you there," said the Headmaster. "And there is no indication what brought this on?" he asked the doctor.

The twins slipped away and hid while they listened to the conversation.

"We found her this morning, wandering across the grounds in her nightgown muttering in that odd language. We brought her here and checked her out. She had fresh wounds on her back, which we treated. Then a little later this morning she began to scream, rant and thrash about. So we had to lock her in the padded room," the doctor explained.

"Any chance she was mauled by a wild animal, possibly infected with rabies?" the Headmaster asked.

"Her wounds would indicate that an animal with sharp talons clawed her back. Once at the hospital, we will test for rabies and other contracted diseases that would cause delirium," the doctor said.

Trinity and Nicholas slipped down the hall and out the door. They walked silently analyzing the situation.

"Wild animal?" Nicholas asked, disbelieving.

"No," Trinity responded.

"Rabies might explain a lot..." he began.

"Except for that voice that we heard come out of her forced open mouth," she interrupted.

They walked back to their class bewildered.

14

Chapter Four

Riley and Anthony met the twins at lunch. Each plopped their tray down on the circular table. The twins told Riley and Anthony what they had seen. Riley had a hard time believing it and immediately bought into the rabies story.

Anthony was a little bit of a geek with massive amounts of useless information.

"You said she recited the children's song, "Ring around the Rosie?" he asked. The twins nodded.

"But she added at the end of the rhyme, 'all because of me'," Nicholas said.

Anthony, the walking encyclopedia, explained that the nursery rhyme originated in England, 1665 during the Great Plague. Children would sing the song. "Ring around the rosy" was in reference to the little red rings that the plague caused on the skin. "Pocket full of posies" referenced to the satchels of herbs and flowers they would wear around their necks because of the smell of rotting flesh. And of course the last phrase, "Ashes, ashes we all fall down" described the death and cremation of all tens of thousands of bodies.

"Ophelia was using her finger nail to carve a little round circle on the top of her hand," Trinity offered realizing the significance.

None of them knew why she ended the rhyme with, "...all because of me."

Riley, innocent as usual, piped up, "She is going to be fine. They will give her something to fix her and she will be back here within a week."

Trinity looked at her naive friend, gently placing her hand on Riley's arm.

"Riley, she isn't coming back. Something is very wrong with her. Something medicine can't fix."

"And I bet those four new students have something to do with it," said Nicholas. As if on cue, the four Dark Ones entered the cafeteria in unison. A small gust of wind entered with them, and Trinity smelled the faint scent of wet animal. The four Dark Ones looked over at the twin's table. Ivy stared down Nicholas with a reptilian glare. She parted her lips and let her forked tongue slip out, like a snake smelling its prey. Roan, ogled Trinity. She turned from his lusting eyes, refusing to look back as the hair on the back of her neck bristled. The four Dark Ones sat with Sabrina and Cole.

The twins and their friends tried to ignore the stares from the enemy table.

Why is Cole hanging out with those guys?" Anthony asked, bewildered. "He was always such a great guy. Now he's become like them, cold and hard."

"He's still a leader, look at their table. It's full of students that want to be near him," Trinity remarked.

"They don't adore him like they used to. Now they fear him," said Dakota, who had snuck up behind Nicholas during their conversation.

Dakota was Nicholas' girlfriend. He and Dakota had met over the summer while both families were vacationing in the Hamptons, New York. They soon discovered that Dakota would be attending Shadowland Academy; a "pleasant coincidence" according to Nicholas.

Dakota's family was from London. Trinity loved her accent. She smiled and scooted over to let Dakota sit by her brother. Dakota and Trinity were kindred spirits in a way. Riley was a little jealous of Trinity's new-found friend. And it did not help matters that Riley looked very much like the plain girl-next-door while Dakota looked like a fashion model. She had beautiful brown, highlighted hair, with green eyes and a perfect complexion. Trinity always teased Dakota that she was fergalicious.

Nicholas told Dakota what they encountered that morning. She listened stunned at hearing about the second trip to the infirmary. When the twins finished their tale Dakota stopped, mid-bite, with her spoon poised in the air.

"Maybe its witchcraft?" she asked.

Trinity shrugged. She wasn't educated in such matters. All she knew was what she had seen in movies and read in books. And who knew if any of that was even true. It could all be fictional, stories from the minds of enchanted writers, weaving tales to intrigue readers.

"The idea fits, in a way," Nicholas said. "Those four have dark auras."

"And the voice coming out of Ophelia's mouth is so Exorcist horror flick," Dakota added.

The five friends ate the rest of their lunch in silence.

Chapter Five

After school Trinity took her snowy white guitar, slung it over her shoulder and walked to the woods. Sometimes when things got hairy, she liked to clear her head by writing melodies and lyrics.

Once far enough from the grounds where no one would hear her, she sat against a birch tree, and began picking a haunting tune. She hummed along, slowly letting lyrics fall from her lips. Before she knew it she was repeating the chorus and working on a second verse. Her crystal angelic voice sounded pure and perfect out in the woods. She liked the solace and comfort she found in nature. She found joy and satisfaction when she created something beautiful with her own voice and talents.

Trinity scrunched up her nose, the smell of wet dog accosted her nostrils. She stopped playing and listened closely. She could hear the crunching of the leaves underneath several sets of boots.

She spotted the Dark Ones tromping through the woods and she crouched behind a large rock for cover.

The steps came closer. They were headed straight toward her. Beads of sweat formed on her forehead and she debated whether to make a run for it. Maybe they had heard her and were coming for her. Maybe they would turn her into a mumbling doll like they had Ophelia. She did not know if she should stay or go. She crouched, frozen in place.

The crunching stopped. She did not dare look over the rock she was hiding behind; the Dark Ones were so close.

"How's our progress?" Zoenn asked.

"He's coming along," Ivy said. "His wounds are festering."

"We must make sure he doesn't turn back, he is our Chosen One. We must see this through." Zoenn urged.

"Do you really think he has what it takes to do what will be required of him?" Roan asked.

"He has been chosen and we must not fail," Zoenn snapped angrily. "It only takes a small turn of events for a person's life path to completely change. We have waited almost a century for another leader like this. If we do not control him, he will be against us and not with us."

"We cannot fail as we did twenty years ago. It is time to rain down genocide as we did through Hitler." Marquis added with a cruel smirk.

"We will not fail. He has almost turned," said Ivy.

"Perfect," Zoenn concluded. The foursome walked off, boot crunching the dry leaves.

Trinity's heart was in her throat as she listened to the conversation. Once she was sure they were gone she jumped up, flipping her guitar onto her back as ran to her dorm.

As she was running she saw her brother come around the corner at a gallop. She ran straight to him. He appeared anxious.

"What's wrong?" he asked.

"Where were you going?" Trinity asked.

"I knew something was wrong, and I was looking for you. Now what's wrong?"

"I heard Zoenn and the other Dark Ones talking in the woods," Trinity said. She told Nicholas everything she saw and heard.

"Who do you think they mean by Chosen One?" Nicholas asked.

"Cole Hopkins," she replied. "Whatever it is, they are grooming him for something bad, really bad."

Obviously. What kind of people plan a genocide or want to be the next Hitler? Bad people.

The siblings walked back to the dorm together. They agreed to meet their friends at dinner time to talk about everything Trinity had heard.

Trinity went to her room, grabbed a towel and her shower kit. She needed to take a hot shower, rinse the sweat from her back and regroup.

As the hot water streamed over her head and down her face and back, Trinity tried to put some of the puzzle pieces together. Zoenn and the Dark Ones had come here to recruit Cole Hopkins to be something or someone very evil. But why Cole? He was such

21

a good kid, and everyone liked him. He was a natural leader and until this past summer, with the divorce of his parents, he had generally always been in good spirits.

That's the answer, she thought to herself. He is a natural leader and people are drawn to him. Maybe his parent's divorce was the turning point in his life. He had two paths he could follow. Each one a complete opposite of the other: one for good and one for bad. Hitler or Gandhi. And the Dark Ones were trying to urge him down the Hitler path.

"I have to warn him," she said out loud.

"Warn who?" Ivy hissed from a couple feet outside of Trinity's shower stall.

She had not seen her come in the bathroom. Trinity thought fast.

"Tell my brother about the pop quiz in Chemistry tomorrow."

Ivy eyed her suspiciously and licked her lips with her forked tongue.

"Good to know," she said.

"Just a rumor, but better prepared than not," Trinity said weakly.

Ivy turned and walked out of the bathroom. Trinity sighed with relief. Goosebumps formed on her forearms and the hair on the back of her neck tingled. She shivered in the hot shower. Evil lingered. Trinity turned the shower off, dried and dressed in fresh clothes. She did not vary her wardrobe colors much. She kept it simple: black, white, gray and red. She never had to worry about something not matching.

As soon as she was dressed she headed over to the dining hall. Her brother and their friends were gathered at their usual table. Dinner was served family style. It had a certain formality to it here at Shadowland Academy.

Nicholas relayed everything that Trinity had experienced that day. Then Trinity added the part about the creepy bathroom experience with Ivy. Everyone was rapt with interest. They spoke in hushed tones.

"Does anyone else think this all getting a little sci-fi?" Riley whispered.

"Not sci-fi as much as maybe Blair Witch," Dakota said.

The biggest question on everyone's mind was who were these four students? Or more importantly, what were they?

Chapter Six

Trinity and her brother were left the dining room, she looked back to see if the Dark Ones were still there. She noticed the dark wood, burgundy tapestries and elaborate chandeliers. Despite the oddities around school, she still appreciated the historic atmosphere. Zoenn and his buddies were not in the dining room. As she thought back, she did not remember seeing them at all.

The sky was dark, the fog was creeping in. The campus was always lit in a way that emphasized the gothic architecture. The group was headed back to the dorm's commons room to discuss what to do. Nicholas and Trinity held back for a second and let the others go inside. She wrapped her arms around herself, chilled.

"Can you feel it too?" Nicholas asked his sister.

Trinity nodded.

"Something bad…" began Nicholas.

"…Tonight," she finished for him.

"Maybe we should stay on watch."

"I don't want to be the next Ophelia," she whispered.

"I won't let that happen," he assured. "But we can't let something else happen, especially since no one else seems to care."

"I feel…" he started

"…a duty, an obligation," Trinity finished again.

"Maybe we can stop it."

"I don't know how, but I hope so," she said.

The two went inside.

After everyone had gone to bed, Trinity and Nicholas met up in the back corner of the great hall where they always met in the middle of the night to talk. They were dressed in black, and ready to sneak around searching out what evil the Dark Ones were up to tonight.

"Ready?" Nicholas whispered.

"Not really."

"Still want to go out?"

"Yes."

The two snuck out of the building and crept around the back corner.

"Where too?" she asked.

"I feel like we should go this way," he gestured.

"I feel like I need some holy water or garlic around my neck," Trinity whispered hoarsely.

Nicholas chuckled, "I don't think they are vampires, sis."

"I don't know what they are, but I'd feel better armed with a priest and a slayer."

Suddenly, the two heard a deep bass drum sound through the woods. Adrenalin pumped through their veins. Their little adventure just got real.

"This way," he said as the two of them rushed toward the sound. They heard it again as they came upon a small stone building half buried into the hillside, at the back of the school property. At the front, was a large wooden door with iron hinges and an old handle. Nicholas carefully opened the door. There was a dark hallway with a warm light at the end. The twins crept quietly along the stone walls. They could hear the deep thumps of a drum beating slowly. Trinity's pulse quickened. Her palms began to sweat. It felt like they were sneaking up to their own execution.

"Cole Hopkins, do you invoke the power and vow to join us," they heard Zoenn bellow. Trinity and her brother looked around the corner. There was a circular room, lit with old-fashioned fire sconce lamps. Pillars circled the room, leaving the outskirts in darkness. Cole Hopkins was kneeling, his shirt off. He did not respond. His eyes glazed over, his face expressionless.

"Drugged?" Nicholas whispered.

"Doesn't seem like he's all there," Trinity said.

Marquis appeared with a branding iron, the one side glowing red, pulled from the stone fireplace. Ivy came to Cole's side and cooed in his ear.

"This will only hurt a little."

Suddenly Roan grabbed Cole's arm and held it out while Marquis placed the red hot brand against the back of Cole's shoulder. Cole screamed out in pain and twisted while Roan held him. Ivy petted his forehead and her tongue snaked close to his ear whispering comfort.

Trinity bit her lip to keep from screaming. She had never been so terrified in her life.

"Initiation…" Nicholas whispered.

"I didn't hear him consent," she said.

The screams stopped abruptly. The branding was finished. Cole had a red welt on his shoulder. He hunched over, drenched in sweat. He heaved from the pain and adrenaline. Ivy bent down to his face and lifted his chin with her fingers. She came close enough to kiss him but instead whispered in his ear.

"You will be a great man, you will serve magnificently."

Cole stared at her. His eyes were wide like he was unaware of his surroundings. She had him in a powerful trance. Trinity wanted to run up and slap Cole. To make him wake up and see what these monsters were doing to him. Nicholas sensed his sister's anxiousness and placed his hand on her arm to calm her.

The four Dark Ones circled Cole, with their arms raised chanting words neither Nicholas nor Trinity could understand.

"The same…." Nicholas began.

"As Ophelia," his sister finished.

As the Dark Ones chanted, Cole knelt in his trance. The twins could not take their eyes off the ritual. They were drawn to the spectacle, the chanting made them drowsy. Trinity thought she

27

nodded off, but then the chants stopped abruptly. She snapped out of it and smacked her brother who also jolted to attention. They had almost been hypnotized.

"It's time," Zoenn said.

"I will bring the sacrifice," Ivy said as she wondered down another hall in the opposite direction as the twins.

"Please Nicholas, I can't stay here," Trinity begged.

"We have to see what happens," Nicholas insisted.

"I can't."

"We must."

Trinity trembled. She grabbed her brother's hand, pleading. Reluctantly, he backed away from the view. A chilling squeal pierced the air. Trinity went rigid.

"We have to see," Nicholas insisted stopping his retreat.

Another squeal.

"The sacrifice is ready," Ivy's said, cruelly.

"I can't watch them butcher a pig," Trinity pleaded.

Trinity grabbed her brother's arm and rushed back toward the front door. Her brother had no choice but to follow. The squealing became even more intense as Trinity quickened her pace. By the time she reached the wooden door, the squeals sounded more like screams. Then silence.

She yanked open the door and ran out gasping for air. She could not stop running. She ran toward the dorms. Nicholas followed close behind.

When they reached the dorms, Trinity collapsed to her knees and breathed heavily, her black hair tumbling down around her

28

shoulders. Nicholas ran to her side and knelt with his arm around her.

"You okay?"

She nodded feverishly. She gasped.

"I don't think that was a pig."

Chapter Seven

Trinity could not sleep all night. She tossed and turned and fretted. She felt guilty they had not burst in and stopped the ritual. Somehow she knew they would be dead if they had tried. She could not get the images out of her mind. She feared they would find another student in the infirmary this morning, or that she might wake up one morning, covered in blood and a horse head in her bed like in the Godfather.

Before it was even light she laid in her bed staring into the darkness. Slowly she sat up and hung her feet over the edge of the bed. She dressed in black and white striped leggings, black shredded sweater with a red tank top peek-a-booing from beneath. Her eye make-up was extra dark today. She felt moody today.

Trinity walked outside and into the mist. Before dawn, the landscape was colorless. Trinity liked the gloom, especially today. She sat on a bench by the chapel and watched a white rabbit pad across the grass looking for breakfast.

Trinity thought to herself, "I'm chasing white rabbits down a dark hole, getting nowhere, going nowhere. The madness is taking its toll."

She would have to write it down at some point and use it as a lyric in one of her songs. She felt a Tim Burton version of Alice, in Alice in Wonderland.

"The peacefulness is deceiving," Nicholas whispered.

She had not seen him sit down beside her.

"Deceptive or not, it's beautiful," she said glancing sideways.

"We have to talk to Cole."

"Warn him," she added.

"It might be…"

"Too late," she finished for him.

The twins got up and headed to breakfast. By the time they walked in, the dining hall was buzzing with gossip. The twins went to their usual table and sat with their friends.

"What's going on?" they asked.

"Kara is missing," Riley whispered to the twins across the table. Nicholas sat with his arm around Dakota and looked worriedly at his sister. She stared back at him.

At that moment the Headmaster came into the dining hall and demanded everyone's attention.

"Has anyone seen Kara this morning or yesterday evening?" he asked the now silent crowd. No one said anything. Then Kara's roommate quietly raised her hand.

"She finished her homework last night and then said she was going to the commons room to meet someone."

"Do you know who?" he asked.

She shook her head. She did not know.

The Headmaster told everyone to stay in the dining hall. They were going to take roll call and make sure no one else was missing. Trinity looked over at Cole's table where she saw him with his head down, almost ashamed. The others, Zoenn, Roan, Ivy and Marquis were smug and unsurprised by the morning's events. Sabrina giggled and flirted as if nothing usual was going on.

After the Headmaster left, the room everyone whispered about Kara's disappearance. Dakota leaned on Nicholas' shoulder.

"What's going on here?" she asked nervously.

"One girl goes crazy and then another goes missing," Anthony quipped. Trinity sat silently with one eye on the enemy table. Cole continued stare at the floor in silence. Ivy leaned over and grinned in his ear something flirtatious. She slid her arm through his. He reluctantly gave her a small smile. Then he turned and looked at Trinity. Their eyes locked. She searched, almost pleading to see a hint of the old Cole. There was sadness. Then hardness. He raised one eyebrow and made a kissing motion toward her. She was confused. Roan punched Cole in the chest playfully and nodded toward Trinity as if he was defending his turf. Trinity felt icky.

32

Anthony noticed the exchange and asked, "Those boys bothering you?"

Trinity answered, "I'm fine."

Before she could get another word out Roan was at their table, sitting in a chair turned around backwards and leaning in close.

"How are you doing?" he whispered. She glared back.

"What? I'm just worried about you. All of you," he said looking her up and down. She stared.

"What's to worry about?" she asked.

"All these girls going missing, aren't you worried?" he asked.

"I can take care of myself," she said.

Trinity wasn't sure why Roan was faking concern. Maybe he knew that she knew something was going on. Maybe it was a veiled threat. She stared at him expressionless.

"Hopefully Kara will turn up," he said as he got up, turned the chair back around.

"She won't," Trinity said staring at him.

He paused, turned, looked into Trinity's defiant glare. He glared back. She held his gaze. A tense energy electrified the air. Just when Trinity thought the pressure of the moment was too much, he snarled and blew her a kiss.

"Secret admirer?" Nicholas asked, slightly concerned. His sister had not told him Roan had taken a carnal interest in her.

She shook her head in disgust.

The headmaster came back into the dining hall with several police officers. One of the officers began to take roll call making sure everyone else was present. It took around twenty minutes to

33

get through the entire school roster. When the officers were sure that the only missing student was Kara, they questioned her roommate and then announced that if anyone had information, no matter how small or unimportant, they should come to the Headmaster's office and talk to the police. Nicholas looked at his sister with an eyebrow raised. Trinity what her twin was thinking. They needed to tell the Headmaster what they had seen last night. She nodded in silent agreement.

Everyone headed to their second period classes since they had spent the first period in the dining hall dealing with Kara's disappearance. Nicholas lagged behind with his sister. The two of them decided that instead of telling the police in person what happened they would write an anonymous note directing the authorities to the stone building at the back of the property. They implicated the Dark Ones and Cole. The twins wrote out the letter in simple block letters so their handwriting would not be recognized, then slipped it under the Headmasters office door.

The twins left, nervous that their identity would be revealed and they would be next on the Dark One's hit list. They went back to class and tried to pay attention but could not. How could they? Everyone's mind was asking where Kara was. The excitement throughout the day made the school day worthless.

By the end of the day the police appeared to have left, but the twins knew they were at the back of the property investigating the stone house at the back of the property. The twins went back to the Headmaster's office to ask what they had found.

"It's confidential at this time," was the only answer he gave. But as they were leaving they overheard the police tell the Headmaster that they had found a small sample of blood and were having it tested. Meanwhile they were going to question the Dark Ones.

The twins were relieved that the crime was being investigated, and they did not have to come forward as witnesses. They did not want to get in the way of the Dark Ones.

Chapter Eight

The twins and their friends watched from the commons room window as the four Dark Ones walked to the Headmasters office for questioning. Trinity caught herself holding her breath. She did not know what to expect. She was nervous and relieved at the same time. The grandfather clock ticked each second off. Each second a slow, grueling moment.

The clock chimed loudly startling Trinity. The long "dong, dong, dong" announced the Dark Ones as they exited the Headmaster's building. Their long dark trench coats, cold stares, and regal air made the moment tense and dramatic. Nicholas and Trinity shivered at the same time. The Dark Ones entered the dorms as Nicholas, Dakota and Anthony left the commons room. Riley and Trinity stayed.

Roan entered the commons room, grabbed a book, sat in an arm chair and read silently. Trinity watched him tensely out of the corner of her eye. Twice their eyes met and they glared openly. Roan see to enjoy the moment; he had a devious sparkle in his eyes.

Trinity heard a couple students come down the grand stairs, it was Sabrina and Cole. They headed out the front door toward the Headmaster's office. Riley glanced sideways at Trinity. They were all about to be questioned.

Trinity pretended to watch the trees sway in the wind, but she was really watching the Headmaster's building. She wanted to see how they acted when Cole and Sabrina came out of the building.

"You were right," Roan whispered too close to Trinity. She startled to find that he was sitting on the couch next to her. His stealth unsettled her.

"About what?" she asked nonchalantly.

"Kara," was all he said.

"They find her body?" she asked as if it did not matter.

"No. Blood."

She stared at him as he stared back. He looked away first.

"Hers?" she asked.

He nodded still not looking at her.

"How do you know?"

He looked at her.

"Overheard the police get the results of the blood test."

Now it was Trinity's turn to look out the window. Here she was talking about Kara's death with her killer as if they were talking about the weather. He was so casual about it. But so was she. She was trembling inside; fearful that maybe he knew that she knew everything.

Roan leaned in, his hand reaching for the arm of the couch, blocking her escape.

"How'd you know she wasn't coming back?"

Trinity glared back at him then shrugged without a care.

"Intuition."

"Back off," she said sternly as he was inches from her face.

His hand slipped from the arm of the couch to her leg.

"I like you."

"Well I don't like you," she said.

He smiled out of corner of his mouth; eyebrow raised. He went back to his corner of the couch picked up his book and started to read.

The girls rushed back to their room.

Riley whispered, "What was that all about?"

Trinity shrugged.

Riley grabbed Trinity's arm.

"He was all over you."

Trinity shrugged again.

"He totally has a thing for you," Riley said giddy.

Trinity glared at her friend.

Riley shrugged.

"I'm just saying."

"He's evil." Conversation over.

38

Chapter Nine

By dinner time everyone had heard the news that Kara's blood had been found in an old building at the back of the property. Everyone at the twins' table ate in silence. They had not told their friends what they had seen or the letter they sent to the police. Their lives would be in danger should anyone find out they witnessed what happened.

"You think she's dead?" Riley asked quietly with her head down. Everyone around the table glanced at each other but did not answer.

"I'm just saying she could have just pricked her finger or something."

"I hope you're right," Dakota said.

The Headmaster entered the room escorted by two police officers. Everyone hushed for news.

"I know that everyone has speculated about what happened to Kara," said the Headmaster. "Today has been a devastating day for this school and her family. Blood was found in a stone building on the school property that was determined to be Kara's. Kara has not been found. As of right now the police are not speculating as to whether she is dead or alive. We have questioned many students that might have information but found nothing very useful."

Nicholas glanced sideways at his sister. Her brow knit in confusion. Both twins wondered why the Dark Ones had not been detained longer or why the police didn't find anything that might link them to what happened last night. The twins realized that unless they were willing to come forward and make an official accusation, the Dark Ones would get away with it.

It did not take long to find out that Sabrina, Cole and a couple other kids had sworn that the Dark Ones had been with them all night. The twins' anonymous letter to the Headmaster was rendered useless by their alibi. Not good.

After dinner Trinity and her brother went for a walk.

"What do you want to do?" she asked, her breath fogged in the cold air.

"We can't prove anything," said Nicholas.

She felt her combat boots crunch the frozen ground beneath her feet. Her black and red plaid skirt brushed against her thighs, and the chain looped around her waist quietly jingled. She was glad she had worn her thigh-high socks instead of knee socks. Her short wool jacket was pulled tight around her.

Nicholas took his red scarf and wrapped it around his sister. He turned his collar up on his wool jacket and shrugged down tighter inside it for warmth.

"We are up against something bigger than two teenagers can handle," he said.

Trinity smiled.

"You mean this isn't like some teen movie where two adolescents save the world on their own?" she asked, sarcastically.

He smiled.

"Remind me to run out the front door and not up the stairs when someone jumps out of the closet and starts chasing me with a chainsaw," he joked.

"Is that before or after my shirt gets torn off and I'm running around in my bra and panties?" she laughed.

He chuckled.

"Our own little horror film, eh?"

"It better not die in my underwear," she huffed.

"Slain. Fully dressed. Duly noted. I'll give the director those notes."

They both grinned.

Silence.

Trinity sighed.

"In over our head."

He nodded.

"Whose gonna help us?"

He shrugged.

"Sounds corny, but we need a miracle."

Nicholas stopped walking. He looked sideways at his sister, then looked straight ahead. Trinity followed his gaze. The two of them had walked to the front steps of the school cathedral.

"Really?" she asked, skeptical.

He shrugged.

"Couldn't hurt."

The twins walked inside the warmly lit church. The interior was as magnificent as the exterior promised. The two had been in here many times for school chapel, but never at night. Candles were lit, the stain-glass windows glowed. The atmosphere was inviting and peaceful.

Quietly they walked to the front of the church. They stood side by side staring at the cross in front of them.

"Never prayed much before," she whispered.

"If we need a miracle, historically this is the place to be," said Nicholas.

"Water to wine."

"Making the blind to see."

"Healing leprosy."

"Parting the Red Sea."

"You're right, this is the place to be," Trinity conceded.

Trinity saw a white feather on the step at her feet. She picked it up and twirled it in her fingers.

"Prayer really going to work?" she whispered.

"They say you have to have faith when you pray."

"Faith that it will be answered? Or faith that there is someone out there listening?" she asked looking at her brother.

"Both," he answered with a handsome smile.

Nicholas took his sister's hand and looked up at the cross, silent.

Trinity felt warm. The good kind of warm, secure. She liked it here. For some reason this place encouraged you to open up, to want to call out to a Higher Being.

"We need help," Nicholas whispered into the silence.

Trinity was going to respond and realized her brother was praying, eyes open, focused on the cross in front of them.

"Don't know what's going on. Don't know how to stop it, fix it, or get the right kind of help."

Pause. The candles flickered and wavered, the light embraced the twins.

"Send help...direction...signs...super heroes," he prayed with a smile.

Trinity grinned.

The twins took a moment to pause and consider what they were really asking for then walked out of the church. Trinity still held onto the white feather she had found. Outside they headed toward their dorm. She stopped and her brother continued toward the door. He turned and looked at his sister who was staring at the sky.

"Coming?" he asked.

"In a sec," she said. She looked at her brother, "It's gonna snow."

43

Slight grin.

"Don't stay out too long," he said, anxious for his sister to come inside.

"It's safe tonight…I can feel it," she answered assuring him looking up toward the heavens.

He went inside. She was sure he'd probably sit and watch her from the commons room window just to make sure she was safe. She smiled, knowing her brother all too well.

She lifted the feather to examine it. Soft. Angelic. She noticed a small silver circle toward the tip of the feather. It was just smaller than a dime. Silvery and perfect.

She twirled the feather again in her fingers, looked up at the sky, and raised the feather above her head holding it in the wind. She closed her eyes.

Desperately she whispered, "Please send help."

A gust of wind caught the feather and it twirled up out of her fingers. She opened her eyes and watched it spiral and float higher and higher. She watched until she could no longer see it.

Then, a single white flake floated down and landed on her cheek. She smiled. Her red lips parted as another flake flew down and melted on her warm skin. She loved snow. And somewhere deep inside she knew someone up there in the white beyond heard her.

Chapter Ten

During the night a severe snow storm came in. The first snow of the year. Almost ten inches blanketed the landscape. It was beautiful. Trinity woke up calm and relieved. She looked at the serene winter landscape. A smile stole across her face. She felt joyous. Snow was a warm, fuzzy feeling for her. "Christmas morning" kind-of warm fuzzies.

She dressed for the day, sporting her black and white striped thigh-high socks, black pleated skirt, and white shirt with a black and red tie. She got out her red wool coat. She didn't wear it often, but when it snowed she loved the contrast of the crimson against the white backdrop.

Trinity rushed outside and watched the snow gently falling around her. The branches were covered with inches of white fluff. She could not help but smile.

As she sat on the park bench near her dorm, she tucked her feet underneath the bench and soaked it all in.

Thirty minutes had passed when Nicholas came out of the dorms smiling as he strolled over to the bench.

"Knew I'd find you here."

She looked over at him, giddy, and then looked back at the postcard setting.

"How you feeling this morning?" he asked.

"You?" she challenged back. Trinity knew they were feeling the same way, they always did. For him to even ask was silly.

He grinned wryly at her.

"Good."

"Peaceful."

"Optimistic."

They both sighed.

"Good," she finished.

They smiled.

Students started pouring out of the dorms headed over to the mess hall for breakfast. The twins met with their friends on the way. Everyone was throwing snow balls and in a playful mood. Innocent victims shrieked as they were caught in the crossfire. By the time everyone was in the dining hall, snow was melting all over the floor, heads was damp and smiles were everywhere.

Roan slipped up behind Trinity and leaned over her shoulder.

46

"I hate snow," he whispered. Trinity cringed and scowled at Roan. He draped his arm over her shoulders. She pushed it off.

"Let me guess, you prefer dry heat," she mocked.

"More than you know," he smirked.

"Figures."

He walked off to his crowd, looked back over his shoulder, and winked. Her stomach churned.

"He's so dark and mysterious," Riley crooned, sneaking up on Trinity.

"He's dark and disgusting," Trinity answered, annoyed.

Riley gazed after him.

"Think Ophelia. Think Kara's blood. He's tied to all that. You like death?" Trinity asked.

"Ya, you're right," Riley whined, disappointed. "But man...death is cute."

Trinity rolled her eyes.

Breakfast was served: hot waffles; coffee; and eggs scrambled with cheddar cheese. Yum. The students chowed down, hoping to get a few more minutes in the snow before class. Everyone seemed to have forgotten that Kara was still missing. But deep down, Trinity hoped help was on the way.

Cole was behaving oddly. He took a handful of eggs and splatted them on a geeky student's head. He laughed. Trinity was stunned. She had never seen Cole so outright mean. Zoenn smacked Cole on the back and encouraged his bad behavior.

Cole had changed.

After breakfast students scattered to throw a few more snow balls. Trinity enjoyed the moment before she ran off to class.

Every classroom was distracted. No one could concentrate while the snow flurried around the windows, teasing everyone. The professor left the classroom a couple times. Each time the noise ramped up.

Ivy curled Cole's hair around her slender fingers, teasing him and whispering naughty things in his ear. A couple times he blushed, but eyed her lustfully. Her forked tongue licked his ear a couple times. Trinity shuddered. Zoenn watched over his pupil with approval. Marquis and Sabrina seemed wrapped up in each other, literally. He could not keep his hands off her. Trinity reflected that the whole scene was like something out of a twisted version of Gossip Girl. Meanwhile Roan kept his eye on Trinity. She ignored his stares. There was no way she was going to become a part of the fondling madness.

The Professor returned to the room and order was restored. Trinity breathed a sigh of relief.

By the third period, everyone had settled down. But between classes students still flung snow balls at one another. Trinity came around the corner of one of the outer buildings and found Cole pushing the face of a smaller kid in the snow. The younger kid cried out in fear. The Dark Ones laughed and egged him on.

"Stop!" Screamed Trinity as she ran forward.

No one noticed her until she grabbed Cole from behind and tried to pull him away. Cole shoved her roughly and continued to torture the kid. But Trinity would not let up. This was inhumane and she could not watch it happen.

She grabbed Cole's arm and yanked. Zoenn shoved her hard and laughed, cruelly. He stepped on the kid's back and shoved his face in the snow. Cole laughed. They each kicked the kid a couple times. Trinity yelled and struggled while Roan held her back. His arms were wrapped around her tightly. Trinity screamed out for help. Not for herself, but for the kid whose face was red and swollen from frozen snow. Roan covered her mouth with his hand, his cheek touching hers.

"You can't stop it. Embrace the cruelty," he whispered.

She struggled even harder. He enjoyed restraining her. Controlling her.

"You're sick," she spat before he covered her mouth again.

Everyone laughed. Sabrina's giggling sickened Trinity. She hung on Marquis' arm as they watched the beating. Ivy then grabbed Cole and kissed him while Zoenn held the sobbing kid down with his foot. Sabrina giggled again. The whole thing nauseated Trinity. The whole thing nauseated Trinity like a bizarre scene from an evil circus.

Finally, Trinity broke free from Roan. By the time she came back with a security guard, the Dark Ones were gone. But she found their victim, his face red and his hair wet. He had a bloody lip.

Trinity ran up and grabbed his arm.

"Are you okay?"

The kid shrugged her off.

"What are you talking about?" he asked.

"Zoenn and Cole beat you up!" she said.

"No they didn't," he denied.

"I saw them! I tried to rip Cole off of you," Trinity said exasperated.

The kid looked around nervously.

"No, I slipped on the ice and fell against the building. I don't know what you are talking about," he muttered.

"Don't lie to cover for them!" she almost yelled.

The security guard looked from Trinity back to the kid, not knowing who to believe.

"When you guys have it figured out, come find me," he said as he turned and walked away.

Trinity knew the Dark Ones had threatened the kid.

"Don't be afraid of them," she whispered.

The kid turned and walked away. Trinity's shoulders sagged as she walked back inside to her locker.

Roan brushed past her.

"You can't win."

"Go to hell!" she shouted.

"Been there….love it!" he said in a sing-song voice.

She watched as he jogged to catch up with the other Dark Ones.

Both doors to the school hall flew open. A flurry of snow blew in with four of the most beautiful people Trinity had ever seen. They were radiant. Everyone in the hall turned to look at them. No one recognized them.

The Dark Ones saw them and stared frozen, intent. The beautiful new kids stared back, challenging. The air was tense and heavy and electricity filled the space between the two groups. The Dark Ones looked away first. They walked down the hall pretending to ignore the new kids.

Girls gawked at the new boys. There were three of them. One had dark bronze skin, tight curly brown hair and the most stunning blue-green eyes. The other two boys looked like they could be brothers. One had brown hair with brown eyes and the other had sandy hair and hazel eyes. The fourth one was a girl, and every boy in the school immediately knew they would never forget her. She had dark red hair, almost maroon, that flowed down her back and green eyes. Very green eyes.

Every student with their jaws dropped. Even Trinity stared. She could not help herself. As the sandy-haired boy passed her he smiled at Trinity. Her whole body blushed.

The new kids disappeared into the office to get their schedules. Trinity hoped she shared some classes with them. Somehow their presence was a ray of hope. Hope for what? She did not know. But between the snow, the new kids, and her unusual prayer with the feather, she was confident things were about to get better.

Chapter Eleven

Trinity sat anxious in her fourth period class. She waited to see if one of the new kids would walk into her classroom. Fourth period came and went, but no new kids. She headed to the dining hall for lunch. She knew for sure she would see them there. They had to eat, right?

When she entered the dining room she scanned the tables looking for the beautiful students. They were not there. Her brother and friends were, and so were the Dark Ones. She sat down reluctantly. Deep down she had hoped for something. Like maybe the sandy-haired boy would smile at her again and invite her to sit with him.

"Get ahold of yourself," Trinity chided herself. She was never like this about boys.

The door opened and white snow flurried inside the building as the four new students walked in together. What was it with the snow flurries? All eyes were on them. The Dark Ones just snarled and kept their heads tucked down.

When the four beautiful students walked by Trinity's table, the sandy-haired kid looked right at Trinity. She could barely smile she was so excited. They sat at a table only twenty-one feet and six inches away.

Nicholas leaned over their table.

"I heard they were army brats."

"I hope they're not brats," Riley said, sneaking another peek at the other table.

"It's just an expression," Anthony quipped.

"What are their names?" Trinity asked.

Nicholas offered his knowledge.

"I heard that the girl's name is Alaina. The darker, curly-haired guy is Phoenix. The other two are brothers. Tristan is the one with brown hair and Logan is the one with sandy hair."

So Logan was his name.

Just then, Logan turned his head and looked at Trinity. Their eyes locked. He smiled. She looked away, shy.

"What is wrong with me?" she chided herself. "I am never shy!"

Dakota noticed the exchange between Trinity and Logan.

"Oh, looks like Trinity may have found her first boyfriend," she teased.

"Hush up," Trinity snap back.

53

Nicholas gave his sister a silly grin.

She rolled her eyes and shook her head.

Trinity and Logan exchanged one more quick glance.

Roan sauntered up to their table, grabbed a chair and pulled it up next to Trinity.

"New kids are a bunch of punks who think they are something special," he spat.

"Maybe they are," said Trinity.

He leaned in close.

"You know you want to be with us…with me."

"You repulse me," she said turning away.

He grabbed her arm, hard. He leaned in, teeth clenched.

"You will not…"

"Get your hands off me!" she said loudly as she tried to pull her arm away from him. Nicholas jumped out of his seat and grabbed Roan's shirt, pulling him away from his sister.

"Stay away from my sister," he warned.

Roan scoffed.

"I'm warning you only once," said Nicholas firmly.

By then everyone in the dining hall had turned to see what was going on. Trinity felt self-conscious. Roan was bigger and stronger than her brother.

Cole came over to their table and patted Roan.

"Come on bro, let's grab some chow." The two of them strolled off laughing. Roan looked back at Trinity and blew her a kiss.

Nicholas turned to his sister privately.

"You have to report his behavior. You know the school doesn't tolerate guys acting like that."

Trinity hated confrontation. Reporting would turn into just that, a big confrontation.

Everyone turned back to eating their lunch, but they kept their eyes on the new students, Tristan, Logan, Phoenix and Alaina.

Riley leaned over to Trinity, her gaze locked on the new kids.

"Unobtainable."

"Maybe," Trinity said blushing.

"You interested?"

Trinity shrugged.

"Game plan?"

She shrugged again.

After lunch Trinity headed to her next class. She sat down in her regular seat and thought what had happened at lunch. Roan was out of control and she was going to have to file a report against him.

"This seat taken?" asked an angelic voice beside her.

She looked up. Logan.

"Uh no," she stammered.

Her pulse quickened, then she pulled herself together.

"Army brat?" she asked.

"Something like that."

"Trinity," she offered with her hand out.

"Logan," accepting her hand-shake.

"American," she guessed from the accent.

"You too."

She smiled.

Good first conversation.

After class Trinity gathered her books.

"Next class?" she asked Logan.

"Chemistry."

"World History."

"Too bad," and with that he left the room.

She headed o her next class, grimacing, because she knew Roan would be there. Unfortunately she didn't have allies like her brother or Riley in this class.

She sat down in her chair avoiding Roan's stare. She put her head down and took notes fervently, trying to get through the class without an incident. The class flew by and she rushed out. One more class and she was off to lacrosse practice. Since there was so much snow, practice would be moved to the indoor arena.

Trinity almost leaped with joy when she entered her classroom. All four of the new kids were there. Tristan sat behind her and Logan to her left. Awesome.

"Long time no see," Logan joked.

"Don't know you well enough to miss ya," Trinity teased.

"We should fix that."

"We'll see."

"Ouch," he quipped, pretending to be offended.

"Deterred?"

"Nope. How about dinner, say 6 o'clock, dining hall?" he proposed.

"Predictable."

"Again, ouch."

Trinity smiled.

"I'm bringing a chaperone...several in fact."

"Me too."

They both smiled.

"Dinner then," he finished.

Class began.

Trinity did not hear a word the teacher said.

Chapter Twelve

"See you later," Logan said as they all left their final class. Trinity nodded, containing her excitement.

Once outside, Trinity headed to the indoor arena for lacrosse practice. No one was there. She jogged over to the coach's office. There was a note on the door. Practice was canceled. Her shoulders sagged in disappointment and she turned to leave. Sabrina, the popular blonde stood several feet away.

"No practice?" asked Sabrina.

"Nope," Trinity said as she walked past her.

Sabrina called after her.

"You know Roan likes you."

Trinity looked over her shoulder as Sabrina followed.

"Well I don't like him."

"You're missing out," she called. "They're all amazing."

Trinity turned around.

"Not interested," she said.

Sabrina called out as Trinity walked away.

"You'll be sorry."

"Oh that's original," said Trinity.

She dashed off to her dorm to dump all her books and find her brother. She needed to make sure he and Dakota would sit with her at dinner since she told Logan she was bringing a chaperone. Once she unloaded her books she headed to the commons room. On her way she ran into Nicholas.

"You have to sit with me at dinner. The new kids want to sit with us," she told him insistently.

"Oh, my sister has a date and needs a chaperone," he teased.

"I don't need a chaperone," she said as she playfully shoved him.

"I like the new kids," Nicholas said. "They have something...something special."

His sister nodded.

"I know."

The twins sat down on the bottom step of the staircase in the hall. The floors were black and white checked, the elegant banister circled a beautiful chandelier. Trinity leaned on her brother.

"You think someone heard our prayer?" she whispered with her head on his shoulder.

Nicholas glanced down at her.

"I hope so."

"Me too."

The sat in silence watching the snow out the front window.. There was supposed to be another snow storm this evening. After several more minutes of shared silence, Trinity sighed.

"I need to check on Riley. I heard she was sent back to the dorm with a temperature."

"Want me to come with you?" her brother offered.

Trinity grinned.

"Oh I'm sure Riley wants lots of company when she's looking her worst."

Nicholas smiled, knowing his sister was right.

She got up and headed down the hall. She grabbed a box of Kleenex and brought it into their room.

"I come bearing a gift," she offered the Kleenex.

Riley sat up in bed, red nose and feverish cheeks.

"It snows and I get sick."

Trinity gave her a pouty lip.

"I'm sorry."

"Give me that," Riley said as she grabbed the box and blew her nose.

"You meet the new kids?"

Trinity looked down and grinned shyly. She nodded.

"Details! I need details," Riley insisted.

Trinity sat down on the bed and told Riley of her brief conversations with Logan. Riley salivated over every detail. She was disappointed she was too sick to make the dinner date, but she made Trinity promise to come back and tell her everything that happened.

Trinity patted Riley's hand and headed out the door. She wrapped her crimson coat around herself and headed outside. She took a walk through the snow. She wandered to the back of the property and found herself near the stone building where they had seen Cole branded with the hot iron. There was yellow police tape surrounding the building and it was sealed off. She backed up and turned to walk back to the main school grounds, the snow gently crunching beneath her feet.

Movement caught her attention between the trees in the distance on her left. She stopped to see what it was. In the distance, someone was walking through the trees. With her bright red coat, Trinity's did not exactly blend in. She kept walking toward the main school grounds, she didn't want to get caught out here with one of the Dark Ones. It seemed the other person was veered toward her as they both walked to the main school building. She picked up her pace.

Nervously she shoved her hands in her coat pockets. She kept glancing sideways to see if she could tell who it was. Most likely it was Roan. All the more reason to get inside so he could not do anything stupid.

Trinity was almost to the dorm building now. She turned the corner around one of the outer buildings when someone grabbed her from behind and shoved her against the stone wall. It was Zoenn. His hand held her against the wall.

He breathed fowl into her face and growled.

"What are you doing out by the old stone building at the back of the school property, huh? Pretty little red riding hood shouldn't be out wondering in the woods. Haven't you ever heard of the big bad wolf?"

Trinity stared at him. Silent.

"Well, pretty girl? What were you doing by the old building?" Zoenn demanded.

She shrugged.

"I just wanted to see what everyone was talking about."

"What's everyone talking about?" he asked.

"Kids are saying Kara's blood was found in there."

"What did you think you were going to see out here?" Still glaring at her.

"Not much. Just curious."

Silence.

"What were you doing out there?" she asked.

He snarled. The he let go of her shoulder and stomped away.

Trinity breathed.

She gathered herself, then walked around the building and sprinted toward the dorms. She wasn't going to tell her brother what just happened. He would just worry. Hell, she was worried.

A snowball fight was in progress in the yard. Students were yelling and squealing, delighted to escape a few moments of homework. Trinity ducked and ran for the door. But she was too late. A large snowball smacked her on the side of the head. She vengefully grabbed a handful of snow, compacted it and hurled it at the boy you had hit her a few seconds earlier. Her aim was perfect, man down.

Now she was caught up in the fight. She had joined one side and made a great snow warrior. Even the boys were impressed at her aim.

At the end of the snowball fight the other team surrendered. Both teams looked like drowned rats, but victory went to Trinity's team. She trudged into the dorm building, wet and soggy. Her hair was stringy and limp, and her boots squished as she walked down the hall. As she was about to enter her room, she heard a soft chuckle behind her. She immediately knew that laugh went with Logan's smile. She looked dreadful and didn't want to turn around.

She forced a smile, lifted her chin and turned to find Logan leaning against the opposite wall.

"That's quite an arm you've got there," he complimented.

"Oh you saw that huh?"

"Wouldn't have missed it," Logan said.

"And my prize is a fully-clothed cold shower," she kidded as she gestured to her drenched clothing and wet hair.

"Suits you," he said with a smile.

"Yes I always thought the drowned rat look was my best," she said, sarcastically.

"Brings out the blue in your eyes."

"And the runny eye-liner," she added.

"I like it. See you at dinner."

And he was gone.

She gently bit her red lip as she watched him leave. She took a shower and got ready for dinner. He'd already seen her worst look, now he was going to see her best.

Chapter Thirteen

Trinity did not know if she wanted to be first into the dining hall and make Logan find her table or if she wanted to walk in with her brother and have Logan invite her to his table. But what if she walked into the dining hall and he didn't see her? Or worse, what if he did not call out to her to come sit with him? She played it safe. She grabbed her brother and Dakota and they went to the dining hall a few minutes early. They sat at their usual table.

It did not take long for the dining room to fill up, but no Logan. Trinity was nervous. The entire dining room anticipated the new kids' arrival. Girls eyed the door, guys side-glanced for a glimpse of Alaina.

To everyone's relief the new kids walked in, confident and smiling. Everyone stopped. Alaina, stunned the room with her long red hair and captivating green eyes. One boy remarked she was as pretty as Christmas.

Logan sat down next to Trinity.

"You didn't back out," Logan joked.

Trinity snapped to reality and realized he was talking to her.

"Why would I back out? I eat dinner every night."

He smiled.

"Dining hall, every night, six o'clock…a girls gotta eat."

"Well said," Alaina complimented. She gave a little wave to everyone at the table. "I'm Alaina."

"Trinity."

"Dakota."

"Nicholas."

"Logan."

"Tristan."

"Phoenix."

Introductions were made.

Alaina looked at Nicholas and Trinity, "Siblings?"

"Twins," they both said at the same time. Everyone smiled.

"Who's older?" Logan asked.

"He is." "I am." They both said at the same time. Everyone smiled again.

"Move around a lot?" Trinity asked.

"Once in a while," Logan admitted. "We just came from New Zealand."

66

Deep down Trinity groaned. If they moved around a lot that meant they were not going to be here long either.

Knowing what his sister was thinking, Nicholas asked, "How long you think you'll be here?"

Tristan answered. "We don't know. I'm hoping we are here at least until the end of the school year."

"Ya, I'd like to stay in one place for my entire junior year," Alaina agreed.

"It must be hard to move around a lot. Constantly having to make new friends and then leave them," Dakota said.

"We are each other's friends. But yes you are right, any friends we make we have to always leave behind," Phoenix answered.

Trinity was bummed. But at least they would be around till the end of the school year.

"I saw you with a stick earlier, you play Lacrosse?" Logan asked Trinity.

"Ya, I love it," she answered. "You play sports?"

"Swim team."

Nicholas perked up.

"Me too. You interested in trying out for the team? We have room for one or two more."

Logan nodded as he took a bite.

"I just might."

Tristan playfully hit his brother in the arm.

"You going to have time for a swim meet? We have a lot of school to catch up on."

Logan and Tristan exchanged a look that only Trinity saw. She didn't know what it meant but she noticed.

The group chatted through dinner getting to know one another. Nicholas and Trinity exchanged a look that said they both liked these kids. These new kids were great. They exuded positive energy, they brought laughter and smiles to the group and everyone was drawn to them.

After dinner the new friends were getting ready to part and go finish their homework.

"You eat in the mornings too," Logan asked,

"Eight in the morning," Trinity offered.

"See you then."

Trinity smiled. Second date.

When Trinity, Nicholas and Dakota were alone they talked about the new kids. Each of them had the same feelings. They really liked them.

"There is something special about them," Dakota said.

"I know but I can't put my finger on it," Trinity said, confused.

"They are the exact opposite of the Dark Ones," Nicholas remarked.

"They are…good," Trinity finished.

The trio went their separate ways. Trinity went to check on Riley. She knew if she avoided her Riley would get out of bed, sick or not, track Trinity down, and demand the details of dinner.

The second she entered the room, Riley pounced.

"What happened?"

Trinity smiled, sat on the edge of the bed and spilled. She started at the beginning and walked through each conversation. By the end of the story, Riley was enthralled.

"These guys are even sexier than the Dark Ones," Riley cooed.

"You're twisted," Trinity said. "The Dark Ones are not sexy. There is no redeeming quality about them."

Riley shrugged, "Dark and mysterious has always been intriguing."

Trinity looked at her friend seriously.

"The new kids are mysterious. Zoenn and his friends are dark and cruel. There is a difference."

Trinity told Riley what Cole and the Dark Ones did, pushing the younger boys face in the snow till he was red and swollen. Riley stared wide-eyed. Trinity also told her about Zoenn pushing her against the building as she came back from her walk.

"Weren't you scared?" she asked.

"Not really…maybe a little wigged out," Trinity said.

"Okay, you're right. I admit it, Zoenn, Roan and their friends aren't very nice," Riley said. "Besides these new kids are so much more intriguing," she giggled. "I know you have your eyes on Logan, but Tristan seems awfully available."

Trinity smiled.

"Fickle thy name is Riley."

"Don't throw yourself at him, they aren't going to be here long," Trinity said.

Rile pouted.

"What about you? Logan won't be here long either."

"I am not pursuing him," Trinity objected.

Riley smiled.

"I know, but don't fall for him."

Trinity looked down.

Riley became concerned for her friend. She had never seen Trinity interested in a guy before. Now all of a sudden she was flirting with a guy that was not going to be around for long.

"Trinity, be careful. If they really aren't going to be here long, you'll just get your heart broken."

She smiled.

"I'll be careful. I'm in high school how hard can I fall?"

Chapter Fourteen

The next morning at breakfast Logan and his friends were sitting at the twins table when they entered. Riley was giddy. She could not take her eyes off of them. Trinity sat down next to Logan as if she had been sitting next to him for years.

"I love the snow," Logan said.

"Me too."

"It always seems like the color white makes the whole world hush and be still," Logan said.

"Awfully sentimental for a guy."

"What? I can't notice the weather?" he joked.

"I like that you notice," she teased, nudging his arm with her elbow.

He grinned and looked into her eyes.

"Are we still talking about the weather?" he flirted.

There is that blush again.

Breakfast went well. Trinity tried to send Riley signals that she was coming on too strong with Tristan. But Tristan just rolled with it, the perfect gentleman. She Trinity shook her head and sighed.

During breakfast girls kept walking by their table, trying to make eyes at the new boys. The boys smiled politely, but kept their attention on the girls at their own table.

Roan glared at Trinity as everyone at their table talked and laughed. Only once did she look over and see him seething. She quickly looked away.

After breakfast everyone headed to their classes. Trinity had three classes with Logan. Instantly these became her favorite subjects. She knew it was a girlish sentiment, but she did not care.

Walking through the hall to her locker she saw Roan heading right for her. She quickly grabbed her books and tried to move away from her locker. SLAM! He shoved her locker door closed and blocked her in with his arm. She glared at him.

"Back off!" she spat.

He grinned wryly, licked his chops, and looked her up and down.

She was angry. He had no right.

She stepped into his face, which delighted him at first, and surprised him with a threat. "If you don't leave me alone, I will report you to the Dean. I don't have to put up with being violated and cornered every other day."

He glowered.

"I can do whatever I want. Rules don't apply to me."

"They will if you get expelled," she said.

He laughed wickedly.

"You don't get it, I make my own rules. And if you report me your brother's blood will be found next."

Whoa.

"You're threatening to kill my brother?"

"I don't make threats."

Trinity got the message loud and clear. She and her brother were on the Dark Ones' radar. Her reporting anything just got postponed. She could not risk her brother's life.

After an awkward silence, Roan assumed she got the picture. He backed up grinning.

"I'll see you around," he said, and winked.

Still stunned, Trinity sat with her back against the locker and her books tightly gripped against her chest. Sick. The entire situation sickened her. But she was stuck. Slowly she walked to her next class, dazed and thoughtful.

She did not pay much attention during her next class. Her brother tried to talk to her a few times but ignored him mumbling responses.

After class he pulled her aside, concerned.

"You okay?"

"Ya, ya…just distracted by some stuff," she stammered.

"You always share, sis, what's going on?" he asked.

"Can't read my mind, twin?" she joked.

"Most the time yes, but I'm still a guy, you're still a girl, twin or not."

She gave him a weak smile, and then playfully bumped him with her shoulder.

"I'm fine. Just thought maybe that a big someone out there would respond more quickly to our prayer."

"Maybe he has," Nicholas said.

She raised an eyebrow.

"Not every miracle or answered prayer is obvious."

"The wise brother imparts his wisdom to his little sister," she joked. "You're right."

He put his arm around her and they sauntered off to their next class.

The rest of the day went seamlessly. No more incidents with the Dark Ones and she and Logan continued their banter. But it seemed almost every time she and Logan had a chance to talk, another girl would come up and interrupt them. Trinity thought it felt like an episode from the TV show, The Bachelor, except Logan did not let another girl steal him away. He stayed attentive to Trinity and always had a polite excuse to give the flirtatious interloper.

Trinity admired that quality in him. He showed her that she had his attention and she was important to him.

Later that day when Trinity was walking through the hall, she overheard girls giggling about how charming and cute the new boys were. Part of her was jealous that other girls found Logan attractive. The other part of her was glad the Dark Ones were no longer the center of attention.

Trinity saw Alaina down the hall. She had on a green corset top and black leather pants, covered by a black fitted trench coat that laced up the back. Her red hair fell over her left eye and she flung it back flashing a smile. Trinity smiled back.

Cole was also watching. Alaina caught his stare and flashed him a smile.

Alaina and Cole? Trinity was a little skeptical about that idea. Cole was not a nice guy anymore, then again maybe she could fix him.

After school Trinity headed to Lacrosse practice and found most her team already there. She quickly changed and got on the field. She liked the strategy that went into the game and the athleticism it took to play. It cleared her mind, and allowed her to take her aggression out on the field.

Today Sabrina and Ivy were in a bad mood and they were gunning for Trinity. They did everything they could to trip her, cross-check her or slash in her in the neck.

"Can't get your game together today?" Sabrina called running down the field.

Trinity tried to ignore her as Ivy ran past slashing her on the back with her stick.

"Get your head in the game," Trinity told herself.

They were trying to goad her. She knew it and she needed to pull herself together. They had a big game coming up and she needed to be ready. Big games were imported. Scouts with

75

scholarships attended big games. Trinity wanted to go to Oxford or Cambridge and this was her ticket.

"Logan is bad news," Sabrina breathlessly.

Trinity laughed.

"No, it's your boyfriend who is bad news."

Sabrina glared at Trinity.

"Marquis is mystical and bold."

"If you like him so much, then stay with him and leave me alone."

The girls were headed back to the locker room. Before they reached the locker Ivy called out, "Trinity!"

She turned around to see Ivy thirty feet behind her.

"Why don't you leave me alone," Trinity said.

"It's too late. You just couldn't leave us alone could you?"

Trinity did not know what Ivy was talking about.

"You had to meddle, you had to stop the work we are here to do," Ivy spat.

"I don't know what you are talking about," Trinity said.

Ivy was furious.

"It's your fault!"

Trinity held her ground.

"They came because of you! And now our work is a thousand times harder!" Ivy's eyes glowed. She was seething.

"I don't know what is going on and what you are talking about," said Trinity.

"Yes you do!" Ivy screamed. Her split tongue slithered in and out of her mouth. Her head twitched a few times in rage. Trinity felt out of place. Whatever was happening right now was out of her league. Ivy's fingers began to curl like talons as though she was ready to leap across the distance that separated them and scratch out Trinity's eyes.

"Stay out of this! See now they are everywhere!" She gestured behind Trinity. Ivy's head twitched again and her eyes darted to her left. Trinity looked over her shoulder and saw Logan standing several feet behind her.

Then Ivy jerked her head toward several palettes of folding chairs stacked fifteen feet high. It was just a motion of her head. But the chairs moved as though pulled by an unseen hand crashing down toward Trinity.

Trinity bolted, trying to escape. In the split second before she was crushed she felt her body rolling across the floor. Logan had her wrapped in his arms, safe. When they stopped rolling he leapt to his feet and faced Ivy. She glared back, breathing heavily. Trinity the silent show-down. It was almost as if Logan and Ivy communicated telepathically, because Ivy shouted "Fine!" then wheeled around and left with Sabrina.

"You okay?" he asked.

"Ya, I'm fine. What are you doing out here?" Trinity asked.

"I just came by to see if you wanted to do your homework with me," he said.

"What was that all about?" She asked him, referring to the silent confrontation with Ivy.

He grinned.

"I was just going to ask you the same thing."

"For some reason I think you know more about what is going on than I do," Trinity said.

"I'm new here, remember? Who is she and why does she hate you?" he asked.

Trinity stared at Logan for a long moment. Then she decided to explain. She told him about the Dark Ones. Zoenn, Roan, Ivy and Marquis were new to the school as well. They arrived in late summer. They were mean and cruel and had turned a good kid bad: Cole. She did not talk about the branding ritual that she and Nicholas had witnessed.

Logan listened intently.

"They sound like disturbed kids if you ask me."

"It's more than that. They're...well, they're evil," she said.

He leaned toward her.

"Evil huh? Maybe you shouldn't hang around them then."

She laughed sarcastically.

"Yes I just love hanging around them all day long," she added after a pause. "I avoid them, but they seem to always find me."

Logan casually hung his arm around her shoulders and started to lead her out of the sports arena.

"Well you should just stay away from them."

She shrugged, "I'll keep trying."

He dropped his arm and shoved his hands into his pockets. The two of them walked back to the dorm building, grabbed their homework and met in the commons room. Logan really did not seem to need as much study as Tristan alluded to earlier. He knew the answers to all the questions. Intelligent. Trinity liked that.

While they were studying, Phoenix came in and told Logan that he was needed. Logan apologized and excused himself, leaving Trinity to wonder where the two of them where going in such a rush.

Chapter Fifteen

Dinner came and went. There was no sign of the new kids. Logan and his friends did not come to dinner. Trinity was disappointed. What was it that had come up that had taken Logan and his friends away from dinner?

Trinity also noticed that the Dark Ones were not at dinner. Odd. Her brother gave her a knowing look. He had noticed the absences as well.

After dinner, Trinity and Nicholas met. She told her brother about what happened that afternoon at Lacrosse with Ivy and Logan.

"You think they know each other?" he asked.

"I don't know if they have met before, but it seemed like they...I don't know, they were communicating on another level. There was some sort of understanding between them."

Nicholas looked at her. Trinity looked at Nicholas. They smiled. Each knew what the other was thinking.

"Meet me back here in fifteen minutes. It's cold out and I need my wool coat," Nicholas said.

Trinity smirked. She was thinking the same thing.

Fifteen minutes later the twins met back by the door, bundled up and with flash lights. They sneaked out to search the grounds for the new kids and the Dark Ones. Both sensed something was going on and as always, they had to find out what.

The twins walked around several of the buildings looking and listening. While they were circling one of the buildings close to the woods Trinity hushed her brother.

"I think I hear something, listen."

The two of them listened quietly and sure enough they heard voices. The twins turned off their flashlights and crept toward the voices. They knew they were close when they approached a large rock formation. They inched around to the side of the rock and could see a circle of people.

Trinity gasped. There, gathered together were all four Dark Ones and the four new kids. Trinity's heart sunk, were they all the same? Were the new kids the same as the Dark Ones?

They listened carefully and Trinity soon realized that the two groups of kids were not the same. They were arguing.

"You will release him!" Phoenix said firmly to the Dark Ones.

The Dark Ones smirked.

"He is not yours to manipulate. He is protected," Logan argued.

"He is ours!" Zoenn growled.

Trinity and Nicholas looked at one another. Who were they talking about?

"We will not let you alter his life path," Tristan said.

Instantly the twins knew they were all talking about Cole Hopkins. They had heard words like that before from the Dark Ones. "Life path" was a word they had used referring to Cole.

"It is too late," Ivy sneered. "His path has been altered."

"He still has time. There is always time to change for the good," Logan insisted.

"He is ours! You cannot change him back," Zoenn said with an evil laugh.

"I demand that you let him be, that you release him or there will be consequences," Tristan threatened.

"It's too late," Ivy sneered.

"We won't let him proceed even if we cannot be able to save him," Phoenix insisted.

"We know that you won't kill him. We have all been here before and we know that you are not authorized to take his life," Zoenn said, confidently.

"We will use other means to stop you. We will not let him go down the path you have designed for him," Phoenix said.

Logan spoke up again.

"I am telling you one last time, release him to us. Leave this place and you will be spared."

"He is ours!" Roan spat.

"He is not. We are here to make sure you do not succeed. You will not succeed!" Tristan shouted.

"If you fight us, it will be your demise. Now leave our presence!" Logan said.

The Dark Ones shifted, agitated. The new kids stood confident and strong, challenging them to make a move. Finally the tension broke as Zoenn tucked his head and led his crew away from the meeting place.

Trinity breathed a sigh of relief. The argument had been tense and she had feared a physical fight would break out.

The four new kids were left in the forest with Nicholas and Trinity watching from behind the rock.

"Put on your armor boys because this is going to be a messy fight." Alaina said.

They left the forest and headed back to the school grounds. Trinity and Nicholas stood in the cold trying to figure out what had just happened. Obviously the Dark Ones were here to recruit Cole to become some major bad guy that would cause great genocide. But now the new kids showed up to stop them.

"Are they all from some secret society like the Free Masons or something?" Trinity asked.

Her brother did not have an answer for her.

"Should we ask them?" Trinity asked.

Her brother thought about it for a moment.

"Not yet, let's see how it plays out."

Something dawned on Trinity.

"Maybe they're the answer to our prayer," she whispered.

Nicholas looked at his sister.

"Maybe….just maybe."

Chapter Sixteen

The next morning the new kids ate breakfast with the twins. The conversation did not include the previous evenings' events. After breakfast, everyone scattered off to their classes. Trinity watched Logan intently when he passed Zoenn. Logan challenged Zoenn with a stare, but the Dark One kept his head down ignoring him.

Between classes Trinity saw Alaina talking to Cole. She wondered what their plan was to get Cole to switch back to his old self. Maybe they were just going to befriend him and convince him not to go down that road. Trinity did not understand what was going on an. What did they mean when they talked about altering his "life path?" She understood enough to know that, in the end, Cole could end up being a good guy or a bad guy.

"Trinity," Alaina called out to her, still talking to Cole. Trinity nodded and walked up to the two of them.

"I was just telling Cole we should all go sledding later. You interested?"

Caught off guard, she stammered, "Uh, ya sure, that sounds like fun."

Cole was smiling. Trinity wondered if he even remembered that just a few days ago she had tried to stop him from torturing a younger kid in the snow. He was smiling and acting like nothing had ever happened.

"We can all meet after class by the gazebo," Alaina said.

She flashed Cole a big smile and teased, "Don't stand me up," and walked off to her next class.

"See you later," Cole said.

Trinity stood baffled.

Later, in class, Trinity was working in a small group with Alaina and Logan.

"How do you guys know Cole?" Trinity asked. The two new kids exchanged a look and then Alaina answered.

"I just met him. But he's pretty cute and seems nice."

"He used to be a great kid. But this past summer his parents split and ever since then he has really changed," Trinity explained.

"How so?" Logan inquired.

Trinity knew he already knew the answer to that question but she played along.

86

"He's been hanging out a lot with those other kids, the ones that have been causing a lot of problems around here. He's really turned into a pretty cruel guy." She told them about the Cole bullying the younger student.

"Maybe we can change all that," Alaina said.

"How's that?" Trinity asked, curious.

"People tend to behave like the people they associate with. So maybe if he hangs around people like all of us, he might change," Alaina suggested.

Trinity looked doubtful. The Dark Ones held Cole under some kind of spell. It would take more than some wishful thinking to undo everything they had done.

"Trust me, it will all work out," Alaina insisted.

"Hope you are right, because if he keeps going down this path, I'd hate to see what he's like when he's an adult," Trinity said.

After lunch the Headmaster announced that there would be no more classes for the day. The faculty needed to meet and discuss some important findings regarding Kara, the missing girl.

Students cheered at their freedom. The four new kids, Trinity, Nicholas and Cole headed out to go sledding for the afternoon. Cole and Logan had found some inner-tubes in a shed and the guys were hauling them up over their heads as the group climbed the big hill. When they got to the top, several of them piled on the tubes and went sliding down the hill. They spent the entire afternoon sledding. Logan grabbed Trinity, pushed her onto an inner-tube, jumped on and the two of them went flying down the hill. They hit a huge bump and the two flew off the rubber and landed sprawled out in a pile of fresh snow. Logan crawled to where Trinity lay in the snow. The two laughed.

"I didn't see that coming," he said, light-heartily.

"You and your brother are close, aren't you?" he asked lying on his belly tracing his finger in the snow. She looked over at him, from her back and nodded.

"We're twins. We can't help but be close. We understand one another. We can feel each other's emotions. We finish each other sentences. It's uncanny."

"I've heard about that with twins," he said watching his finger trace the snow.

She rolled onto her side, resting her head in her hand.

"It's nice always having a best friend like that."

Logan nodded.

"Are you and your brother close?" she asked.

"Tristan and I? Ya, we're close, but not where we can practically read each other's thoughts like you and Nicholas."

"Sometimes it's not great," she said rolling her eyes.

Logan chuckled.

"No privacy?"

"Exactly. He always knows when I'm feeling bad, or something's wrong."

The two of them talked as the sun moved toward the horizon. The sky glowed different colors. It made the snow look luminescent. Breath-taking.

Trinity smiled at Logan. She looked at his flawless face, sparkling eyes and sighed. He could not be any more perfect. She lay on her back and started making swinging motions with her arms and legs. Then she stood up and looked at her handy-work.

"What's that?" Logan asked, standing close to her.

"A snow angel," Trinity answered.

Logan looked deep into Trinity's eyes. Understanding.

"You could be one, you know," she teased.

"A what?" he said, his mouth dry.

"A snow angel."

Silence as he searched her eyes.

"Because you are practically perfect," she teased, shoving him into the snow as she took off running.

He jumped up, laughing, and took off after her.

As the sun set, Trinity's snow angel glistened in the twilight while laughing students rushed past without a notice.

Chapter Seventeen

When Trinity entered the dining hall, she saw Cole and went to talk to him.

"That was a lot of fun today," she said.

He smiled back.

"It's been a while since I've hung out with you and Nicholas."

"I heard there was going to be a game night in the commons room tonight. You interested?" Trinity asked.

"Ya, that sounds like fun," he said.

Nicholas walked up and gave Cole a fist pump. The new kids entered the dining hall, but the Dark Ones were nowhere to be found.

Logan told Cole he should eat with them. He agreed. The group sat down and had dinner together. It was times like this that Trinity thought Cole seemed more like his old self. Once in a while she would see darkness or a dead look in his eyes. But it seemed like the new kids were winning him back.

After dinner they met in the commons room and had fun playing board. It felt like old times. Everything seemed to be going well. Trinity started to feel like maybe everything would be fine after all. No need for a super-natural, super-hero intervention.

At the end of the evening everyone said their goodnights and planned to meet again for breakfast.

Trinity lay in her bed, relaxed and happy that things were getting back to normal.

In the morning, Trinity got ready in her usual black, white and red clothes. She didn't bother pulling back her hair. She let it hang unruly down her back. She hummed a little tune that had come to her the night before. When she had free time she would go to the woods and write lyrics to go with it.

Trinity entered the dining hall smiling but immediately sensed something was wrong. Cole was sitting with the Dark Ones and Ivy had her arms wrapped around him. The new kids were at the twin's usual table, but other kids were standing in groups and the room was buzzing.

"What's going on?" she asked her brother.

"I think they found Kara's body" he said.

She sat at their table, glancing at Cole. Apparently he had regressed and was ignoring the twins and their new friends. The room hushed as the Headmaster and several police officers entered.

"Everyone take a seat," he ordered.

Silence.

"The police have concluded after a thorough investigation that Kara is dead."

The room buzzed again.

"Everyone please quiet down. I know this is a shock for many of you and we have counselors that you can talk to if you need to," he continued.

"There will be an investigation and everyone will be asked to cooperate. All of your parents have been informed. As of now, they are ruling her death the result of a wild animal attack."

The new kids looked at each other, skeptical. Trinity rolled her eyes at her brother. He silently nodded.

"We don't want anyone out after dark. With the animal still out there it is too dangerous and we want to make sure it does not happen again. We are also asking that everyone walk with a buddy, no one walking alone. Is this understood?"

The students all nodded. The Headmaster and the police left the room and everyone began to talk at once. Boys were excited at the prospect of a wild animal out there, girls were scared and nervous.

"Walk with a buddy? Is that so you can push your 'buddy' down so the animal can get her and give you time to make a run for it?" Dakota joked.

Logan looked at Trinity, who looked skeptical.

"You don't believe him?"

Trinity shrugged, "I don't buy it."

Tristan eyed her carefully, "What do you think it was?"

Trinity looked at him and weighed her answer, "I think she was murdered."

"You think someone here at the school killed her?" Alaina asked.

Trinity shrugged. Nicholas gave her a warning look. He did not want her sharing too much. They did not know these new kids that well and somehow they were involved. The twins needed to keep their secrets till they knew who they could trust.

"I don't know what I think," she backtracked. "I've been out in the woods a thousand times and not once seen any animal that could kill a human."

"I'm sure they will figure out what it was that killed her. There probably really isn't too much to worry about," Nicholas said, ending the conversation.

The conversation turned to more pleasant matters and no one addressed why Cole was not sitting with them this morning.

After breakfast everyone headed to their own classes. Trinity was leaving the dining hall when she bumped into Cole.

"Hey Cole, how come you didn't sit with us this morning?" she asked, casually.

He kept his head down and left the building without uttering a word. Trinity stood there, books in her arms, watching him jog away. The snow swirled around her as she kept her eyes on Cole till he was out of view.

"Cole is with us now," she heard a seething voice from behind her. She looked over her shoulder to find Roan hovering.

"If you want to spend time with Cole, you have to spend time with me," he said.

She laughed. "Ha. I'd rather eat dog poop."

"That can be arranged," he said.

She glared.

"What do you want to hang around with those new kids for?" he asked.

"I like them," she said, matter-of-factly.

"We can offer you so much more than they can," he crooned.

She looked at him quizzically.

"I see you noticing everything that is going on. You are curious and have questions. I have answers," he enticed.

"What kind of answers?" she asked.

He smirked.

She raised her eyebrows…waiting.

He chuckled, put his arm around her and started to lead her to their first class.

"Hang around and you'll find out."

Trinity forced a laugh. "Not on your life," she said as she walked away.

Roan stood in snow looking after her. She did not dare look back.

Later, during one of their classes, Trinity tried to talk to Cole. He gave her the brush-off. Ivy gave her a satisfied look. They had said something to Cole and now he was avoiding the twins and the new kids like the plague.

Roan cornered Trinity again, "we aren't that bad, you know."

He oozed a sleazy charm.

She looked at him, disgusted.

"We could enlighten you, show you things you've never seen before," he said.

"I bet!" she sneered sarcastically.

He laughed.

"Where do you know the new kids from?" she asked.

"What do you mean?" he asked, carefully.

"You knew them before they came to the school, right?" she asked, not leaving room for him to wiggle out of the question.

"No, not really," he said.

"I see the way you look at one another. It's like the Capulets and Montagues from Romeo and Juliet," she said.

"We don't like them, they don't like us," was all he said.

For the first time, she seemed to have rendered him speechless. She did not want to let up, but she did not know how to proceed without revealing that she and Nicholas had seen them in the woods a few nights ago.

He changed subjects. "Cole is with us because he has seen what we offer. He has been enlightened and has a new wealth of knowledge. You could have it all too. I have seen your potential."

She stared.

Silence.

"I'm offering you a chance to change your life," he said.

Trinity was curious. What could they have that she did not know about? A secret society? Every movie she had seen about secret societies, bad things always happened.

The offer hung between them. She saw something enticing in his eyes and yearned to know what it was. It felt like Eve standing there staring at the apple. Bite or no bite? But in the end it did not fare well for Eve. Trinity concluded the consequences might outweigh her curiosity.

"Forget it," was her final answer. She walked away.

Chapter Eighteen

The rest of the day was uneventful. By evening Trinity and Nicholas were finishing up their homework and headed off to bed. While she was in her room changing into her pajamas she saw movement outside her window. She stopped, turned her light off and watched out the window. She saw four figures in dark trench coats headed to the woods.

Her heartbeat quickened. Was that the Dark Ones or the new kids? She could not tell from the window, but she knew it must one or the other. She ran to get her brother, but did not need to go far because he had seen them from his window and was coming for her.

"Another midnight trek?" she asked.

"Ya think we're gonna get eaten by wolves?" he answered.

"I'm more likely to believe vampires at this point," she said, sarcastically.

"What about werewolves?" he said, smirking.

She rolled her eyes and through on her coat.

They ran into the woods as quietly as they possibly could. They saw a light ahead and followed. It was not the yellow beam of a flashlight. It was a bright, white light. Whatever it was, the four mystery students were following it.

The twins followed close behind, until they all came to a stop.

The foursome gathered around what seemed to be a white, round rock about a foot in diameter. Trinity could see that is was Logan, Tristan, Alaina and Phoenix. She was relieved. Odds were she and Nicholas were safe out here.

The four new kids stood in a circle, their arms wrapped around one another's shoulders, heads down. They were talking, but too quietly for the twins to hear what they were saying.

"What do you think they are doing?" Trinity whispered to her brother.

He shrugged.

The bright white light started to shine, from the midst of the group of four. The light began to expand until it formed a column that extended up to the heavens. It was white and silver with hues of blue.

The foursome seemed to be communicating silently with the light and to one another. They almost seemed to be "charging up" and gathering strength from the light.

"They seem to be communicating silently with each other," whispered Trinity.

"It's almost like they are communicating with that bright light as well," said Nicholas.

"This is way too sci-fi, it looks like they are gaining strength from the light," said Trinity.

The twins stood nervously in awe of what they were watching.

"It's beautiful," they said in unison.

Then the light faded and the four bowed their heads in the circle. They spoke one word in unison, which the twins could not quite hear, then broke their huddle. They walked back past where the twins were hiding. The twins crouched as low and out of sight as they could and watched as they four new students walked by, heading back to the dorms.

The twins followed from a distance.

"I didn't expect that," Trinity said.

"Okay, I almost would have bought into the idea of werewolves and vampires, but not aliens," Said Nicholas.

"I don't think its aliens."

"How do you explain that bright column of light shooting up into the sky?" he asked.

She thought about it.

"Heavenly."

"This is getting bizarre," Nicholas said.

"Yes but not once did I feel unsafe," Trinity said.

"Me neither."

"We need to do some research."

"On what?" he asked.

"I don't know. Super-natural stuff. Aliens, vampires, superheroes, I don't know. You prayed for a superhero, maybe that's what you got," she said.

"Whatever it is, I think it's other-worldly."

"Well it's not Superman."

"Tomorrow."

"Tomorrow," she agreed.

The twins went back to bed. Neither would get a wink of sleep after the night's events. And how in the world was she going to face Logan tomorrow and not reveal that she had watched them.

"Poker face," she kept telling herself. "Poker face."

Chapter Nineteen

It was early morning. Trinity had not slept for even ten minutes, so while it was still dark she dressed and walked through the cold to the school library. She kept thinking through all the possibilities of what she saw last night. She planned to browse through the index to see if the library had any answers.

The school's library was extensive. It was three stories high and was the second largest building on campus. When the school was founded, the library and its contents were donated by a generous benefactor who wanted the young scholars to have all of the knowledge of the world at their fingertips. That was before Google.

Trinity typed away at the computer, looking through book summaries and indexes. She was not looking for generic books on "UFOs," she was looking for something specific, though she did not know what. Possibly something about rituals or paranormal beings. Her eyes stumbled across a book titled, "The Ancient Struggle: the Beings of Darkness and Light." That caught her attention so she looked to see where in the library the book was located.

Restricted.

The book was in the restricted area of the library.

The restricted area was a section that was off-limits to students. It took a password to get through the locked, glass doors. The title intrigued her. She knew it would have answers to what she was looking for. The question was how could she get access to the book?

She went to breakfast crush pondering her predicament and barely noticed when Anthony, Riley's secret crush, stumble up to her table and sat down.

"What's on your mind?" he asked.

"I need to access a book in the restricted section," she said, immediately regretting saying it out loud.

"Piece of cake," he said, happy he had the answer.

"You have access?" she asked.

"No, but I can get access," he said.

"Anthony, don't tease. It's electronically guarded..,.how?"

He smiled.

"I just happen to be a genius code breaker."

"You're a hacker?" she asked, surprised.

He grinned sheepishly.

"How come you never told me?"

"You don't exactly go around announcing to the world that you're a hacker," he said, in a hushed voice. "And I've never hacked anything important. But I don't think hacking into the school's library is going to get me into much trouble. So when do you want to go?"

"Tonight!" she said, excited. "I want to go tonight. Let's go right before closing. That way the alarm won't be on and the librarian will be busy getting ready to close. We can even bring Riley and Dakota to distract the librarian."

"Brilliant," he said.

The new kids were not at breakfast, which gave Trinity and Anthony time to explain their mission to the rest of the table. Riley and Dakota agreed that they would distract the librarian while Anthony, Trinity and Nicholas broke into the restricted section to retrieve the book. After school they would meet in front of the library to execute their mission.

Trinity watched all day for the new kids. She wondered why they were not at breakfast. She was not sure about anything anymore. Maybe they had been taken home on their mother-ship for all she knew. She was hoping for a more logical, preferably human, explanation.

"Having a crush on an alien isn't very appealing," she thought to herself, grimacing. Then she smiled and said out loud, "of course, the idea of a super hero is a little more attractive!"

During one of the later classes the new kids made their appearance. Trinity was unusually quiet. She did not want to say anything. She feared she would give too much away if she said anything. It was better to keep her mouth shut.

"You're awfully quiet," Logan said.

She shrugged, still quiet.

"Something wrong?" he asked, genuinely.

"No," she answered, avoiding eye contact.

"Did I do something? Did I offend you?"

"Of course not."

He was clearly concerned at her silence. So not wanting him to get the wrong idea, she tried to come up with something to explain her behavior.

"I just have a lot on my mind and we have several tests coming up and I'm still trying to get a scholarship from Lacrosse so I can go to Oxford. It's all piling up this week," she blurted, trying to cover up the truth.

"Why do you need a scholarship?" he asked. "Parents that send their kids to Shadowland Academy don't usually have a problem paying for an expensive university."

Suddenly he felt rude.

"I am so sorry," he said. "I didn't mean to pry into your family situation."

She smiled, her mood softening.

"My parents will pay for half of my college education, but they feel that I will appreciate it more if I also pay for half. That means I have to get a job, a good one, and earn scholarships to pay for my half of the tuition. A Lacrosse scholarship would really help to cover my half."

"Ah, smart parents," he remarked.

She returned the smile. Paradise was restored.

All day, Trinity could only think about the book that she was going to smuggle out of the library. She went through the plan a gazillion times in her head. Then her mind started considering all the theories and explanations for what she had seen last night.

By the time school was over she was jacked up on adrenaline. The group went into the library. Riley and Dakota carried out their plan to keep the librarian busy and the twins and Anthony went to the restricted section.

"Do you know where it is?" Nicholas asked.

"Generally," Trinity answered.

Anthony pulled out a small electronic device and connected it to the alarm pad on the door. Once inside they would have to move fast because the restricted section was set apart from the main library by one long glass window. Anyone in the library could see them inside the restricted area if they decided to look.

Anthony's device beeped and the door opened. The three slipped inside. Trinity led the way, searching for the row where the book was located. Finally she found it. She was nervous and sweating. Her fingers ran across the bindings of the row of books, looking for the title. She stopped at a very large, thick, book with a hard leather binding. The book appeared to be hundreds of years old. She pulled it out, thumbed through it and knew she had what she needed.

"Got it!" she said, excited.

"Let's get out of here," Anthony said as they had already started to jog for the exit. Trinity just hoped the book didn't set off an alarm as they left the restricted area. She could not read the whole thing here; a volume this large was going to take her a long time to read.

They raced through the glass door, shutting it on their way out. No alarm sounded. Once in the safety of the unrestricted part of the library, Trinity put the book in her bag and walked calmly out the front door. She felt guilty and excited at the same time. She had never stolen anything before. She kept telling herself they were just borrowing it, because she had every intention of returning it. It was a library, after all.

Trinity knew they could not sit around and read this book in the open, so she and her brother went back to her room and began looking through it. It was full of historical information throughout the centuries. It had witches, demons, angels, super-natural beings and rituals she had never heard of.

Trinity was intrigued by a section on warrior angels. It showed drawings of the angels' bodies, marked with unique and distinct tattoos. The markings covered their sides, part of their back, half their arms and one of their shoulders. She thought the tattoos were beautiful, even stunning. Each warrior angel had similar markings but no two were ever the same. The tattoo symbolized an allegiance to a legion of warrior angels whose job was to fight the forces of evil and darkness.

"That's pretty cool," Nicholas remarked about the tattooed warriors as they kept thumbing through the book. Trinity was looking for something about ceremonies or rituals with beams of light, but did not find anything. She still had more than half the book to thumb through but they needed to stop and get their homework done. Trinity hid the book in her room. The twins planned to read more later.

After they finished their homework they had a school party to attend. Every year the school celebrated Roman history with a toga party. The twins had almost forgotten in their excitement to read the book, but tonight was the celebration.

"You have your costume?" Trinity asked her brother.

"It's a white sheet. How hard could it be?" he joked.

They parted ways and went to get ready for the party. Trinity was glad she was not on the decorating committee, because she would have had to be there three hours early. She would never have had time to go through her new book. Luckily her brother was right. A white sheet and some gold cord, was all she needed to skate through the front doors of Rome.

Trinity got nervous thinking about Logan being at the party. She was still enamored with him, even if she did not know what he was. How could anyone not be captivated by him? He was perfect. But maybe that was what was wrong with him; he was perfect and possibly not human. She kept telling herself there was a logical explanation. If not then maybe he was some sort of super human. By the time she was ready to go she was so nervous she had to physically calm herself down in front of the mirror.

"Snap out of it Trinity," she warned herself in the reflection. Her black hair contrasted with the white sheet. She was showing off some leg and a bare shoulder. A gold cord looped through her hair, Roman style. She smiled at her reflection. She was ready to go.

She met her brother downstairs and they traipsed over to the dining hall laughing and joking about last year's costume debacle. One of the freshmen had worn a white sheet like everyone else, but his was a little on the thin side. Instead of wearing white, he had worn red underwear. Everyone could see his bright spanks underneath his costume. He had been a good sport and laughed about it, but it would always be remembered.

As they neared the hall, they could hear the music and festivities. Students were laughing and having a good time. Everyone was decked out in costumes. The hall was illuminated and decorated from top to bottom. The school always went all-out for parties and festivals.

Trinity linked her arm in the crook of her brother's and the two entered the hall. Quickly she scanned the crowd looking for the mysterious Logan while Nicholas could not take his eyes away from Dakota. Trinity rolled her eyes at him and gave him playful shove toward his girlfriend.

Before she could find Logan, he had found her. He offered her a glass of punch. He had come ready to partake in the tradition and was dressed in a toga. He looked charming and handsome. His freshly-showered sandy hair, was wispy and a couple of locks curled on his forehead.

Some rowdy kids on the dining hall balcony yelled out to Logan. He raised his glass to them and they cheered. Trinity was glad to see that the new kids were quickly gaining popularity. Logan and Trinity small talked. Tristan and Alaina joined them. Tristan hung his arm around Trinity's shoulders.

"I knew I'd find you two together."

Trinity raised one eyebrow. Was Tristan alluding to the idea that Logan always sought her out? She liked the idea.

The small group spent the rest of the party together. Trinity melted each time Logan flashed her a charming smile. His perfect teeth, his sparkling eyes. He really got to her.

Later Trinity saw Alaina talking to Cole. He seemed to be enjoying himself. She looked around for any of the Dark Ones but she did not see them. Trinity wondered if Alaina was using the opportunity to try to sway Cole. Alaina looked over at Logan and gave him a nod. She wondered what that meant. What was Alaina signaling?

A little later Logan excused himself, and he and his brother went outside. Trinity went to find her brother. Something was going on. She did not see Alaina and Phoenix anywhere and the Dark Ones still had not shown up.

"You think they are meeting again?" Nicholas asked his sister.

"Something is going on and I don't know what."

"Alaina was with Cole earlier. Did you see that?" he asked.

"Yes, and she gave Logan a nod. Like something was going on."

Trinity and her brother went outside to search.

Meanwhile, around back of the dining hall, Logan and his friends were having a serious talk with Cole.

"The choices you make today will affect the rest of your life," Tristan told Cole.

"Zoenn and his friends are bad news, Cole. Don't listen to them," Phoenix encouraged.

Cole just stared at them.

"We've known Zoenn a long time and he has a way of messing people up," Alaina said.

"I'm sure you've seen his powers."

Cole nodded once and looked away.

"He has dark, evil powers that come from a bad place," said Tristan.

"I think I'm in too deep," Cole said, quietly.

"It's not too late," Alaina urged him.

"I've made my choice," he said, unconvincingly.

"Just think about what we've told you," Logan said.

"You don't have to make your choice today. Look deep inside yourself and think about what you know is right."

Cole turned away sheepishly.

Just then, the Dark Ones strode around the corner. They intimidated in their black trench coats. Their appearance was sharp and somber. They were clearly unhappy that the new kids had Cole.

"Look what we have here," Zoenn said in a cruel voice.

"Leave our friend alone," Roan threatened.

Ivy curled up next to Cole, seductively sliding her hands up his arm and caressing his shoulder.

"Don't touch him," Logan ordered her.

She grinned a wicked grin.

"I know what you are doing," Logan said. "Take your hands off him and let him choose for himself."

"What am I doing?" she said, innocently.

Silence.

Logan glared, threatening.

"Fine," she shrugged, taking her hands off him.

Cole did not understand anything that was happening, but he watched intently. When Ivy took her hands off him he felt different. She always seemed to have an emotional grip on him. Maybe that was because she had some sort of magic touch.

"Cole, come with us," Zoenn said.

"You don't have to go with him," Logan argued. "We can protect you."

Cole just stared at the two groups. He did not know what to do.

Zoenn stepped closer to Cole.

"You know what you need to do," he said in a low voice.

The air was tense. The new kids looked ready to make a move. The Dark Ones stood ready for a fight.

"You are with us," Roan said with a hand on Cole's shoulder.

"I am with them," Cole said, almost in a trance.

"Release him," Tristan threatened.

Roan just grinned.

111

"Release him," he warned again.

Roan smirked.

"Make me."

Tristan stood up to his tallest and the new kids all poised to strike. Everyone tensed. Silence.

Alaina placed a hand on Tristan's forearm.

"Now is not the time."

Tristan looked down at her, relaxing a little.

"Now is not the time," she repeated.

The new kids relaxed. They knew they would have another chance. Alaina was right, everything had to be done at the right time. Cole had to make the choice on his own. They backed away and left.

Trinity and her brother practically ran into the new kids at the front of the building. They had not seen the stand-off that had just transpired between the new kids and the Dark Ones. They had been searching in other areas of the grounds for the meeting they knew was taking place.

"What's going on?" Nicholas asked, nonchalantly, as if he hadn't been hunting for them.

"We're headed back to the party," Phoenix said, ushering the twins toward the dining hall. Trinity and her brother exchanged a look. Something had happened and they had missed it. Logan saw the look between the twins, but did not know what to make of it.

"I'm pretty tired," Trinity said. "I think I'm going to call it a night."

112

Logan offered to walk her back to the dorms. She nodded shyly. The two of them strolled back to the dorm.

"I'm glad you're here at Shadowland," he said, quietly.

She glanced over at him.

"I didn't expect to meet a friend," he added.

His words were a little confusing. Why wouldn't you assume you would make new friends when you transfer to a new school?

It was as if he heard her thoughts.

"We usually transfer into a new situation and transfer out before we've gotten to know anyone." Pause. "You're different. I noticed you immediately."

She was tickled to hear him say so. She had noticed him as well; so had every other girl in the school.

"I can't explain it," he said. He looked at her sideways. He seemed baffled by his own feelings.

"I noticed you too," she said.

He smiled as if he knew that everyone noticed him. It was not a smug smile. It was an all-knowing smile. He knew that people noticed him and he was not arrogant about it. He was almost embarrassed.

He stammered.

"You don't understand, I...I don't notice..." then he stopped trying to find the right words.

He tried again.

"It has never happened to me before."

Trinity stared at him. She did not know exactly what he was saying. She thought maybe he was trying to explain that he had never had a crush before. Or maybe he was trying to say that Super Heroes or whatever he was do not fall in love with mortals.

He shrugged.

"Whatever it is, I like it."

Trinity smiled. Quietly he slipped his hand over hers. She felt warm and safe with her hand in his. They walked in silence to the front of her dorm. The evening was peaceful. The snow was silvery in the moonlight. No words were needed. She smiled at him, said goodnight, and walked into the building.

When she got to her room she looked out the window to see Logan walking in the snow back to the dining hall. It was a beautiful picture.

She undressed and curled up on her bed with the borrowed book from the restricted area of the library and thumbed through it again. She studied the section about warrior angels with the body markings. They truly were beautiful. She fell asleep with the book in her hands, dreaming of snow angels.

Chapter Twenty

Trinity had been thinking about the book and exploring the possibilities. She had a theory and she wanted to run it by her brother. After school she headed to the school's indoor pool. Her brother was on the swim team and he had practice this afternoon. She entered the Aquatics Center. Nicholas was in a 100 meter relay. She watched as he finished. A couple of the guys waved at her. She smiled back. As she waited for her brother to finish she glanced at all the pennants on the wall. Shadowland had won championships four years in a row and had a solid history of taking home the trophy even before that.

Trinity noticed Logan in the coach's office talking with him. She strained to see the front of his face. The glass walls were frosted up to about his shoulders and then clear from the shoulders up. Logan was partially facing away from her. The coach shook his head and shrugged his shoulders. Logan looked upset. Trinity moved into better position to see Logan's face. She had forgotten about her brother.

Logan and the coach came out of the office and Trinity immediately looked away and pretended to not see them. She tried to find her brother so she could pretend she had been watching him the entire time. But she could not help herself. She looked over at Logan, who was in his swim shorts. He was muscular and naturally tanned. Her eyes moved from his well-cut abs to an elaborate tattoo he had on his front left chest over his bicep and shoulder. As he walked closer her mouth gaped open. She could feel her heart race and she could not take her eyes off the markings on his body.

Logan spotted her, smiled, and trotted over toward her. She could not make eye contact. She could only stare at the tattoos on his body. She had seen them before; just last night, in fact, in her book.

"Hi," Logan said softly.

She could not utter a word. Her mouth opened but no words came out.

Just then Nicholas walked up behind Trinity.

"Hey sis, what are you doing here..." his sentence trailed off as he recognized the tattoos on Logan's body.

Logan seemed uncomfortable with their stares.

116

"Coach says the school has a 'no-visible tattoo policy', so I can't be on the swim team," he explained, confused by their gawking.

"Oh ya, that's too bad," Trinity barely found her voice.

"Cool ink," Nicholas choked out.

"Ya, really unique and beautiful. I've never seen such good work," she added.

"I'm going to go get dressed. Maybe I'll have to take up Lacrosse," Logan joked as he jogged off to the locker rooms.

Trinity looked at Nicholas, wide-eyed.

"No. Way."

"Holy..."

"Stop! Holy...yes...holy something...but don't... just don't swear," she said as if Logan could hear them.

Nicholas chuckled.

"This is amazing," he said stunned.

"Do you really think it could be?"

"What else would it be? he asked.

"They are exactly the same."

"Ya. I know."

"Wow."

"No sh..."

"Nicholas!" both Trinity and the coach yelled at the same time.

Nicholas winked at this sister and ran over to his coach.

Trinity watched him and then headed out of the Aquatics Center. The cold, crisp air hit her and felt good compared to the muggy, humidity inside the pool area. She sat on a bench and pondered what to do.

"How can it be?" she asked herself. "I don't really even know if I believe in…angels." She could barely get herself to think the idea let alone say it; but she knew what she had seen. Logan had the same markings as the book she had been reading last night. Logan was a warrior angel, if the book was right.

"Maybe someone's just playing a prank on us," she thought.

Deep in thought she barely heard Logan walk by her. He did not see her sitting on the bench.

She stood.

"I know what you are!" she blurted out.

He turned, confused.

"Hey Trinity. I didn't even see you there."

She did not walk toward him; she just stood there staring at him. He stared at her. Silence. Logan acted as though he had not heard her. But she knew he had.

"I know what you are," she said again, softly.

He jerked his head a little, concerned. Then he smiled calmly.

"What? I'm a swimmer-turned-Lacrosse player?" he joked.

She took two steps toward him.

"I've seen your markings before…in a book."

"My markings?" he brushed her comment off and started toward the dorms.

She followed twenty feet behind.

"I know what you are," she said again.

"I don't know what you mean," he said over his shoulder and kept moving.

She followed him.

"I'm the one that called for you to come!"

She stopped moving. He stopped walking.

He turned to look at her. Inquisitive. She stared back. All was silent again.

She was breathing deeply. She was nervous and scarred and putting it all on the line. What if he was not what she thought?

He took one step toward her, wondering if she really did know.

"My brother and I prayed for help...whatever that may be," she explained. "They're out of control and we didn't know what else to do."

Logan stared, searching her eyes.

She took a chance, "There was a...."

At that moment, he took out her white feather and held it between his fingers.

"...a feather," she finished, astounded.

The two of them closed the ground between them and were suddenly standing inches apart. Their warm breath fogged the crisp air.

"Are you really an ang....." she started.

"...angel," he finished for her.

He nodded, smiling down at her. A huge load had just been lifted off his shoulders. He had an amazing connection with her, something he had never experienced with a human before. He was drawn to her. Compelled by her. He could not stop thinking of her. He needed to be near her, and yet he had a secret he had to keep. But now she knew. She had been the one to ask for help without even realizing what she had been asking for.

"So what are those other kids?" she asked concerned.

"Who else knows?" he asked her, without answering her question.

"My brother."

"Meet us back in the woods by the triple rock formation," he told her.

Without even thinking she asked, "You mean where the four of you met and that white light thing...."

The look on his face made her stop.

"You've been spying on us," he said a wry grin.

Sheepishly she shrugged.

"Yes, meet us there in twenty minutes."

They looked deep into one another's eyes and there was a wave of strong emotion. He grabbed her hand and squeezed.

Then he ran off in the opposite direction and she went back into the Aquatics Center to get her brother.

Trinity was excited, scared, nervous and in awe, all at the same time. When she ran into the center she nearly collided with her brother.

"They are...I talked to him...you won't believe it...I can't believe it...but it's true....they came....we prayed..." she rambled.

"Slow down! What's going on?" he said, actually understanding everything she had just blurted out.

"They're real," she said out of breath, a smile creeping across her face.

"Wow."

She nodded.

"How?"

Trinity dragged her brother across the school grounds out to the forest and explained as they jogged. By the time they reached the designated spot, he had been fully briefed.

Logan, Tristan, Alaina and Phoenix were there waiting for them. Trinity thought she had never seen something so beautiful and strong, and she was excited at the possibilities.

No one spoke at first. Then Tristan stepped forward.

"Logan says you know."

Trinity nodded.

"We're the ones that called or prayed or whatever it's called."

"How'd you know?" Tristan asked.

Trinity explained all that they had seen from the Dark Ones, Ophelia, their suspicion that they had sacrificed Kara, the desperate call for help in the school chapel, and the white feather and prayer in the night. She told them that she and Nicholas had followed them. They had seen the white light and they had suspicions. They found a book that had a chapter about angelic warrior beings with special markings on their body. Trinity explained that they were the same markings that Trinity and Nicholas had seen on Logan at the pool.

Logan seemed ashamed for a moment.

Tristan looked at Logan.

"I told you not to try out for the swim team."

Alaina smiled.

"He can't help himself, you know that."

Tristan explained.

"He loves the water. Our last mission was in New Zealand. Someone saw Logan in the ocean and sworn they had seen a mermaid."

Logan grinned sheepishly and shrugged.

"So you are here to help with the Dark Ones?" Trinity asked.

The foursome looked confused.

She explained.

"Zoenn, Roan, Ivy and Marquis."

"Yes...the Dark Ones as you call them," Tristan said, amused.

Before she could ask what the Dark Ones were, he warned, "You must not speak of this to anyone. No one must know what we are. You must carry on as we have."

"We need to get back before everyone notices the six of us are missing," Alaina said.

Tristan nodded.

The twins walked back toward the dinner hall a different way than the four warriors so they would not to draw attention.

As they were walking in the dusk of the evening, the snow quietly crunched beneath their feet. It began to snow again. Trinity stopped, looked up at the white flurry showering down from the sky and she smiled to herself. She had her own real, live snow angel.

Chapter Twenty-One

Early in the morning Trinity watched out her window as the snow drifted lazily downward. With the new blanket of white fluff, everything looked perfect. She watched in silence. As the sun began to rise, she got dressed. Black and white plaid, pleated skirt, black and white striped thigh-high socks, black boots, white beanie, black and white scarf and her big red wool coat. She grabbed her guitar, a wool blanket and headed out toward the woods.

As the time ticked by she wrote a haunting melody. Her pure voice carried through the drifting snow. The sun began to cast warm hues over the landscape. Trinity stopped singing after she had finished her last verse and chorus. She was giddy about her new composition. She stood up, took several steps into the snow and fell backwards. She made a snow angel, grinning from ear to ear.

SNAP! She stopped, ears perked, adrenaline pumping. Someone was near. She did not know if she should get up and look around or lie perfectly still. She carefully rose to her feet, squatting, staying low.

CRUNCH! Eyes wide, heart pounding, she looked around trying to stay tucked behind a tree. Whoever it was obviously had heard her and must know she was here. Maybe she should make a run for it. She turned to grab her guitar and run. She was still squatting when she found herself staring at black combat boots. She yelped in surprise and fell backwards. When she looked up, she saw the dark, piercing eyes of Roan.

She crabbed-walked back one step and within a millisecond Roan was down squatting next to her, menacing. He lit a cigarette and exhaled the smoke. She sat, leaning back on her hands, ready to scramble away.

"I can't figure you out," he said, casually glancing at her.

She sat silently. Waiting.

He took another drag on his cigarette. She grimaced at the stench. Roan chuckled, licked his lips, and looked out through the trees thoughtfully. Then he turned his focus back to Trinity.

"You don't like me much do you?"

She stared, eyebrows raised. She glanced around trying to plot an escape.

He leaned forward, rotating his head around hers to get her attention and make eye contact.

"Trinity," he whispered her name slowly, bewilderment in his voice.

He smirked, still holding her gaze.

"T...R...I...N...I...T...Y," he whispered hoarsely drawing out her name even slower than the first time. There was a pregnant pause.

"I can get anyone to like me, but not you."

Another drag on his cigarette.

"Why is that?" he asked quietly, almost as if he was asking himself and not her.

He flicked his cigarette off into her snow angel. Trinity rolled her eyes at his lack of respect for the environment. His trash and black ash destroyed the beauty of the white snow.

He placed a hand on her knee, looking at her for a response.

"Do you not feel that?" he asked, confused.

"Your hand?" she spat.

His brow furrowed.

"No...more than just my hand. You don't feel...enticed?"

"I feel your cold clammy hand and that is all."

They stared at each other in silence.

"Nothing? No feelings? No urge to act or feel a certain way?"

Leaning closer to his face, she threatened, "The only thing I feel urged to do is kick the crap out of you."

He chuckled, amused, yet befuddled.

"Amazing...it's like you're immune."

125

While Trinity did not know exactly what he was talking about, she got the feeling he expected her to feel more when he touched her. She had seen Cole become entranced when Ivy crawled all over him. Maybe they had powers over people when they touched them?

"You're the first...to resist," he told her.

"You're evil, I know you're evil and I want nothing to do with you," she whispered harshly.

"And that makes me want you even more," he mused.

She gave him a hard kick in the chest. He fell back into the snow laughing. She grabbed her guitar and walked back to her dorm. She glanced over her shoulder once to make sure he was not following her. He stood on the edge of the birch trees watching. He lit another cigarette. She was confident he would not follow her.

Once inside the safety of the dorms, she went to the restroom to make sure she was presentable for school. She stood starring into the mirror.

"Why can't I feel it?" she asked herself. "What am I supposed to be feeling when he touches me?" A small smile crept across her face. She had a power, the power to resist whatever the Dark Ones were emitting. She nodded at herself, assured.

As soon as she entered the dining room, Roan glanced her way and gave her a nod of recognition. She feared that he was going to continue to make advances. Since she was immune to his supposed charms she was that one thing he could not have. Of course that made her the one thing he wanted. She was prey, a conquest, a game to win.

126

A warm voice broke her thoughts.

"You going to sit down? Or stare all day," Logan joked. She smiled at him and sat down glad to be near him. She had not completely worked through her feelings regarding the situation.

She had a crush on an angel.

"Brilliant," she thought to herself. "How's that going to work out for you?"

Logan slid his hand over hers.

"You okay?"

She sighed and tried to come back to the present.

"Ya, I've just been processing a lot," she answered.

Sheepishly, he slid his hand back.

"I know."

They looked at one another realizing their relationship could not go anywhere. The rest of the table ignored the two of them while they contemplated their predicament. Tristan eyed his brother, wondering how he could have fallen for a human. He had tried to warn his younger brother, but there was no stopping him. He was head over heels for this girl. He was under her spell.

Trinity had a lot of questions for Logan, like what their plan was and who the Dark Ones were. But her questions could wait.

After breakfast, Logan took her by the hand and the two of them ran off to spend their Saturday getting to know each other better.

Once they were out of everyone else's hearing range, she leaned on a birch tree and asked, "How old are you?"

He looked at her amused.

"Well?" she implored.

"I don't really know," he answered, grinning.

Her eyebrows raised, head tilted. She was not sure if she believed him.

"I was created before the universe," he offered, apologetically. "I was created before time was born," he shrugged as he tried to explain.

"You were created? You didn't just exist?" she asked, curious.

"I was created just like you. But we are different...um...species, I guess is how I can explain it."

She wanted to know more, she was trying to understand. At the core of her curiosity she needed to know if they could somehow make it work.

"I don't know," he said, as if reading her mind.

She stared at him.

"Can you read my thoughts?" she thought to herself, testing him.

He smiled.

"No I can't read your thoughts."

"Really?" she said, out loud not believing him.

"Really," he assured her.

"Then how?" she asked, pressuring him.

"I was just thinking the same thing," he whispered, stepping closer, and taking her hand in his.

She looked down, then back up at him, sending a silent prayer that it could work.

"Now I heard that," he whispered.

"How?"

"You prayed it," he murmured as he leaned in and gently kissed her on her crimson lips. Her breath sucked in as they kissed. Her body felt warm and tingly. It was magical.

When their lips parted he whispered, "You've been kissed by an angel."

She ran her fingers down his perfect face, smiled at his cheesiness.

"My snow angel," she breathed. He grinned.

They spent time walking and talking. He held her hand.

"What are they?" she asked.

"The students you call the Dark Ones?"

She nodded.

"Just that. Dark Ones, Fiends, Ghouls, Daimones, Demons, whatever you want to call them. Humans have called them different things throughout history," he explained.

"Do they have powers?" she wanted to know.

He did not answer her right away.

"Do you have powers?" she asked.

He looked at her and hesitated.

"We all have powers of sorts," he finally answered.

"Do they have powers to turn or persuade when they touch a human?" she asked.

"Have they touched you?" he asked, wondering where this was going.

She nodded.

"And I didn't feel anything."

He looked slightly bewildered.

"Then why do you ask?" he inquired gently.

"Because I've seen others...respond...to their touch," she tried to explain.

He nodded.

"Touch is powerful."

She understood. And yet she was confused why she hadn't felt anything when Roan had touched her.

"You didn't feel anything?" he asked.

She shook her head. He smiled.

"Maybe you have powers of your own," he joked.

"Do you have powers through touch?" she asked.

"It's different. We touch to comfort, to assure, to heal and bring peace. We believe in freedom of choice."

She understood the difference. She also knew he was not telling her everything. He could not tell her everything, and she knew she would never understand it all. She was not meant to. That was what made the idea of him enchanting and magical.

Sitting up on a large black rock, she asked him about their plan, what the Dark Ones were doing here and what they wanted from Cole.

"The Dark Ones have come to alter Cole's life path," Logan explained.

"Life path?" she asked, even though she thought she knew the answer.

"You make choices that direct your walk in life. Cole has a great destiny should he make the right choices. But the potential that we see in him for good, they also see potential for evil."

"So they want to alter his path so that he uses his potential for something bad?" she asked.

"Exactly."

"How bad?"

"Ever heard of Hitler?"

"They want him to be the next Hitler?" she asked, unbelieving.

He nodded and shrugged looking down at his hands.

"Genocide...persecution...war...destruction."

"What if he chose the other way? What kind of good would he do?" she asked.

"He'd stop it, prevent it. Be the hero, instead of the villain."

"Wow," was all she could whisper.

How mind boggling it was that small choices in his life could lead Cole down two completely different paths. Giving in to the pressure, making one bad decision after the next, Cole could become the villain in his own story instead of the hero.

"If you believe in letting him decide for himself, then how are you going to persuade him to make the right choice?" she wanted to know.

"Right now, the Dark Ones have their claws in him and he is not able to make his own decisions with a clear head. We need to remove those pressures and let him make decisions for himself.

We are confident without Ivy and Zoenn poisoning his mind he would make the right choices."

Trinity listened to everything Logan had to say. She could see what needed to be done, but she did not know how they were going to do it. Was there going to be a big fight? Were they going to be able to persuade him to not listen to the Dark Ones and make his own decisions? What was the plan and how could she help?

Logan grinned. She did not have to say it out loud, he just knew what she was thinking.

"I'll let you know when you can help," he said.

She glared at him.

"You can read my thoughts!" she spat, half angrily.

He threw his hand up in defense.

"I swear I can't!"

She glared at him playfully.

"I just knew what you were thinking. I promise I couldn't hear anything," he vowed, sincerely.

She tilted her head, looking at him suspiciously.

"I wouldn't lie to you," he whispered, honestly.

She softened.

"You better not," she threatened, playfully.

He leaned in.

"Just be careful what you pray for though."

She smiled and looked deep into his eyes. He was amazing. She was foolish. How would she ever explain him to her parents.

Hey dad, meet my boyfriend, Warrior Angel Logan.

Logan smiled.

She got suspicious.

"What am I thinking?" she asked.

"I don't know. But probably exactly what I'm thinking," he said.

She snickered.

"Complicated."

"Exactly."

With that said, he put his arm around her and they watched the sun set.

Chapter Twenty-Two

Sunday morning Trinity sat in the school chapel in a pew next to Logan. The music swelled while she looked around at the stained glass windows and frescos painted on the ceiling. She grinned at the paintings depicting beautiful angels in white gowns, bright halos and white feathery wings. She looked over at Logan.

"They are so much better in person," she thought.

In one of the paintings there was some sort of creature. Trinity pondered the idea that there were heavenly creatures she could not even fathom.

"Are there dragons up there?" she whispered to Logan. He smiled at her, amused.

"I can't tell you," was all he said.

She glared at him.

"You ever read Revelations?" he asked.

She shook her head.

"Read it and you tell me if it's possible."

She smiled and shook her head in frustration.

A little later she whispered, "It's a little weird that an angel is sitting in church."

"There's nothing weird about it. This is where I belong."

The two listened to the rest of the service.

Afterwards, Trinity, Nicholas, Logan and the others were outside soaking in the sunlight that shown down on the white school grounds. They sat around the stone steps talking.

"So if Cole won't change his course, why don't you just give him measles or end his life in some way to stop a catastrophe from happening in the future?"

"Humans have free will," answered Tristan. "We don't coerce people to make certain choices and we must live with their choices. It's one thing that sets us apart from them."

"You mean the Dark Ones?" Nicholas asked.

Tristan nodded.

"The Dark Ones have altered Cole's life path and have him in their clasp. We are here to release him from their spell and let him make choices without their evil influence," Alaina explained.

The twins understood what they were being told; they just did not know how it was going to happen. They had seen the kind of grasp the Dark Ones had on Cole and it was going to take a war to make them go away.

135

The group decided to head over to the dining hall for lunch. Trinity had to run back to the dorms for a second and grab a hat and scarf. She told them she would meet up with them in a few minutes. Logan offered to go with her, but she waved him off.

She ran to the dorm and was about to leave when she nearly ran into Zoenn, who was leaning in the doorway. Zoenn slightly scared her. He was the leader of the Dark Ones and he was just plain mean. She kept walking toward the door staring at him while she put her hat and scarf on. Just as she reached the door he put his arm across the doorway to stop her. She stopped and stared at him defiantly.

"What do you want?" she asked, tired of their game.

"Give me your hand," he demanded.

"What for?" she asked.

"I'm not going to hurt you. Now give me your hand."

Trinity stared at him for second then put her left hand out. Zoenn took his right hand and clasped her hand, fingers interlaced, palm to palm. He stared at her. She stared at him, waiting. Zoenn's eyes narrowed as he watched her. She could sense that he was fuming inside.

"How do you feel?" he asked.

"Hungry. Now can I go eat?" she answered.

His eyes narrowed again, confused.

Trinity was annoyed.

"You guys are really getting on my nerves. I can't feel whatever vibe you are trying to send to me through my hands. Why don't you leave me alone? You're never going to turn me like you are trying to do to Cole. And I'm not going to let you ruin Cole either."

Zoenn seethed. He grabbed Trinity, turned her around so her back was squeezed to his chest: his hand still grasping hers. With his arm across her chest, holding gripped her tight and close.

He leaned over shoulder and whispered in her ear angrily.

"We may not have power over you, but we will transform Cole into the leader we need him to be."

Trinity was scared.

"You can't stop us!" he spat in her ear.

"I might not be able to stop you on my own, but Logan can," she challenged.

Zoenn was angry and squeezed her tightly.

She winced in pain.

"You are severely mistaken. Your new little friends won't stop us either. We are powerful." he said. "Don't be delusional. Your friends aren't going to win this battle."

She squirmed to try to get away from him, but he held her tight. He quietly chuckled.

"I may not be able to influence you through touch, but I am stronger than you and can influence you by force." he sneered.

"What ever happened to 'I won't hurt you'?" she demanded.

He laughed and released her but still held her hand.

"I won't hurt you now. But you do anything to get in my way and I can't promise I won't hurt you then," he said through clenched teeth.

Trinity just stared at him.

He grinned, wryly.

"You are different."

Pause.

"That intrigues me."

Trinity groaned inside. Just what she needed, another Demon stalking her.

"Are you done?" she asked, starring at their intertwined hands.

He released her hand and let her pass. As she headed through the foyer and opened the front door she glanced over her shoulder at Zoenn. He had vanished.

Trinity hurried to the dining room. She did not know if she should mention her encounter to her brother, or Logan. There really wasn't anything they could do about it. Her brother would just worry and Logan would be angry. She also did not want everyone to get side-tracked. The focus needed to be on how to get Cole back on track, not on her little encounters with Zoenn or Roan. She decided that if one of them hurt her or seriously threatened to hurt her, then she would tell them. For now, she would keep this to herself so everyone focused on the bigger problem: making sure Cole did not become the next Hitler. A little hand-holding from Zoenn was harmless in comparison.

"What took so long?" Logan asked as she neared their table. Food was already on the table and everyone was helping themselves.

Trinity smiled and shrugged. She did not want to tell a lie.

Trinity sat down and started to eat. Her mind wandered to the murals and stained glass windows in the church.

She quietly asked Logan, "Do you guys have wings?"

He smiled and winked.

"What does that mean?" she smartly remarked. "Yes? No? Or I can't tell you?"

Logan grinned and shrugged.

"Logan," she whined playfully.

"What took you so long earlier?" he pried.

She grinned and shrugged.

"Exactly."

Chapter Twenty-Three

Monday afternoon, Trinity was headed to the Lacrosse field. She was in a pretty good mood. She had done well on a couple of tests she had today. As she entered the indoor field with her sticks thrown over her shoulder, someone stepped behind her and knocked her sticks off. She whipped around and saw Sabrina and Ivy standing there.

Trinity didn't want a confrontation so she swung her sticks back over her shoulder and walked toward the locker room.

Sabrina stepped up behind her and grabbed her sticks. Trinity stopped and turned, the two girls hanging onto the sticks from either end.

"What's your problem?" Trinity asked, annoyed.

"You are my problem!" Sabrina spat.

"That's original," Trinity rolled her eyes.

"Ivy said you've been hitting on Marquis," Sabrina explained.

Trinity laughed as Ivy watched amused.

"Why would you tell her something like that?" Trinity asked Ivy.

She shrugged.

"I'm just calling it like I see it."

"Ivy, you're making it up to stir up drama."

Trinity turned to Sabrina.

"What makes you think I am interested in Marquis, or that I even want to talk to him?"

"I've seen you watching us."

"Sabrina, I assure you, I am not interested in Marquis. He is all yours," Trinity insisted.

"Stay away from my man!" she spat.

Trinity looked from a heated Sabrina to an amused Ivy.

"Really? We aren't in junior high. I told you I'm not interested, and that's the end of this," Trinity assured, perturbed with the entire conversation. She grabbed her sticks and headed to the locker room.

"I'll be watching you," Sabrina yelled after her.

Trinity turned around and rolled her eyes. Today would be interesting on the field.

As the coach ran through some drills, Ivy sat on the sidelines watching. Trinity was just waiting for the hammer to drop. She knew Sabrina was not finished with this fight and she was waiting for her to lash out. The problem was, Trinity knew she could

141

handle Sabrina on her own. But she could not battle Sabrina and Ivy together. Ivy was not exactly just another high school student.

Sabrina and Trinity were on opposing teams for the drills. Sabrina was rough and Trinity had to battle intensity with intensity or she would be bruised and beaten. They were tripping, slashing and cross-checking one another throughout the drill. The animosity escalated until Sabrina was blatantly slashing Trinity on her back with her stick. Trinity was smacked to the ground. She started to get pissed off. Sabrina's accusations were false and she was taking her emotions out on Trinity on the field.

Trinity had enough. She stood, threw her stick to the ground and turned toward Sabrina.

"You are out of control!" Trinity yelled.

Sabrina sneered.

"I'm just playing the game."

"You're tripping, slashing and hitting me just to take your out-of-control emotions on me. Get a grip!" said Trinity.

Sabrina shoved Trinity.

"Keep your hands off of me," Trinity warned.

Ivy watched from the sidelines. She loved drama.

The coach noticed the problem and jogged over to the girls.

Sabrina lost control and shoved Trinity harder.

"Knock it off," the coach yelled as she approached.

Sabrina was about to come after Trinity again who was standing her ground, but taking the hits, when the coach stepped between them and stopped Sabrina from taking another whack at Trinity.

Neither of the girls said anything.

"You girls want to tell me what this is about?" the coach asked.

Trinity just stood staring at Sabrina. Sabrina was silent.

"If you girls won't tell me then you better work it out off the field," the coach warned.

"I don't have a problem coach," said Trinity.

The coach looked at Sabrina, questioning. No response, just a blank, cold stare.

"If you have a problem Sabrina, fix it off the field or bury it," coach said.

Cold stare.

"You hear me?"

Sabrina nodded.

"Good. Now let's be a team and get back to work."

The two girls turned opposite directions and went back to their sides.

The rest of the practice was pretty amiable. Once in a while Sabrina threw in a cheap trick to lash out at Trinity. But Trinity was not interested in reciprocating. It would only stir up more problems. Some of Trinity's teammates asked Trinity what the fight was about. Trinity just told the girls she did not really know. Most of the girls quietly told Trinity that Sabrina had been getting erratic and mean. None of them wanted to be the focus of her attacks so they steered clear of her. Trinity thought they were cowards. Everyone should be willing to stand up for what is right, even if it is to their social detriment. Otherwise evil prevails.

After practice Trinity gathered her things and headed back to her dorm. She figured rumor would get around about the fight on the field so she would just wait until her brother brought it up. What was there to talk about really?

At dinner everyone gathered around the table. Nicholas looked at Trinity. She stared back at him. He knew.

"Sabrina thinks I am after her boyfriend Marquis," she told her brother quietly.

Nicholas snorted.

"That's absurd," he said.

"No joke."

"Don't worry about it," he said.

"I'm not."

Dinner proceeded.

Halfway through dinner Sabrina came over to their table. Trinity thought she was going to stir up more trouble for her but she was surprised when Sabrina honed in on Nicholas and whispered something in his ear. Nicholas smirked and shook his head no. Sabrina played with his collar and whispered again in his ear, playing, sweetly.

Nicholas answered.

"Fine." Sabrina walked away satisfied.

Trinity looked at her brother, eyebrows raised.

He leaned over and whispered, "She wants to talk to me."

"That can't be good," Trinity warned.

"Nope."

"Don't let her worm her way back into your affections Nicholas. Please be careful."

"That chapter is closed, don't worry," he assured his twin.

"Don't even let it appear that you are giving her an inch. You don't want to make Dakota feel insecure or you could lose her. And she's worth keeping. Dakota is nothing like Sabrina."

She did not want him to lose his girlfriend because a crazy ex-girlfriend started causing problems. Dakota knew that Sabrina was Nicholas' ex-girlfriend so Nicholas did not have anything to hide.

"Should I not meet her?" Nicholas asked.

"No. And if you feel like you need to, then have someone else there. You don't want Sabrina to say something happened that didn't. You need a witness."

"Smart."

They finished their dinner and went back to the commons room in the dorm. Everyone was working on homework. A few students were reading or playing a game.

"When are you supposed to meet her?" Trinity asked.

"Tonight. Do you want to come with me?"

"Oh brother, do I have to?" Trinity whined. "Because my first choice for entertainment this evening would be to accompany you to a completely awkward meeting with your ex."

Nicholas sighed.

"I'll do it," Trinity relented.

"Thanks."

The two of them excused themselves and went to meet Sabrina. When they rounded the corner Sabrina was not happy to see Trinity.

"What's she doing here?" Sabrina objected.

"You didn't think I was going to meet you alone, did you?" Nicholas said.

"I can't talk about us with her here. It's too private," Sabrina said.

"Whatever you have to say, you can say it in front of my sister. She knows all about us and I don't keep secrets from her." Nicholas said.

"That's a little freaky Nicholas, telling your sister all the details of your relationships. But then again, I kind of like freaky," Sabrina said, seductively.

"She's my twin. I tell her everything that's important. It's not like you and I were married. We are in high school and we went out. Not a lot of private or secret stuff."

"Like I said, I like freaks," Sabrina cooed and stepped toward Nicholas, who shied away.

"Oh, don't play hard to get," she advanced toward him again.

'Don't touch me," he warned.

"Why are you coming on to my brother?" Trinity asked. "Just today you were going on and on about Marquis."

"I realized how much I miss him and I want him back," she pouted.

"That's never going to happen," Nicholas said, sternly.

146

"He has a girlfriend. A nice girlfriend," Trinity added. 'I'd hit him over the head before I let him date you again."

"Ah, you don't hate me that much," Sabrina insisted, playfully.

"Are you bi-polar?" Trinity asked. 'Today you were ranting about me hitting on your boyfriend and now you're hitting on my brother."

"What are you talking about?" Sabrina asked, playing innocent.

Nicholas looked at Trinity and she just shrugged.

"We are done here," Nicholas said.

'No, don't go," Sabrina said with a sad pout trying to be cute.

Trinity and Nicholas turned and left. Sabrina was acting crazy and they wanted nothing to do with that freak show.

As soon as they were out of ear shot, Trinity asked, "What was that?"

"Psycho. Part two," he said.

"Make sure you tell Dakota everything that happened, ok?"

"I will."

"You don't want Sabrina telling another crazy story before you tell your girlfriend what happened. And in the future, don't ever agree to meet with Sabrina again."

"Noted."

"She's bad news."

"I got it."

"Really, really bad news."

"I got it," he insisted.

"I'm just making sure," she said. She smiled and linked her arm in his.

Once back in the commons room, Nicholas told Dakota everything that transpired. Trinity vouched Nicholas' version of the events. Trinity didn't want Dakota thinking for a second that Nicholas did anything inappropriate or that he did anything to betray her trust. Dakota listened and understood. She was thankful that Trinity was there to keep things under control. Who knows what would have happened should Nicholas have gone alone? Sabrina would have been all over him. Plus, if Sabrina starts rumors tomorrow, Trinity can vouch for the actual events.

Trinity was glad the talk between Dakota and her brother went well. She really liked Dakota and she did not want her brother to lose her.

Trinity decided she'd had enough drama for one day and went to her room to finish her homework before bed. Alone in her room, she wondered what was going on with Sabrina. Her behavior certainly was odd. Trinity wondered if it was influence of the Dark Ones or if maybe she really was bi-polar. Whatever Sabrina's deal, Trinity planned on staying as far away from her as possible.

Chapter Twenty-Four

In the morning around the breakfast table the twins told Logan and the others what Sabrina had done. They asked if maybe her behavior was because of something the Dark Ones influenced her to do. Tristan did not know what her problem was.

"Careful Nicholas, she might alter your life path," Trinity joked.

Nicholas playfully swatted his sister.

"She's not going to influence me to do anything except run as fast as I can away from her."

Everyone laughed.

During second period Trinity started to nod off. All the drama was wearing on her and she just needed to close her eyes for a second. She did not know how long she had been napping when she heard the professor's voice.

"Trinity!"

She bolted upright and apologized. The teacher noted that she was sweating and flushed. The professor told her to go see the school nurse. Trinity thought she was okay but she obeyed.

Once in the nurses office, she found out she had a high temperature. The nurse gave her some pills to bring her fever down and sent her to her room to get some sleep.

Trinity lay in bed, shaking from the high fever. She did not feel good at all. She was amazed at how quickly she had gotten sick. She had felt fine that morning at breakfast. Actually, now that she thought about it, she had felt tired. She quickly fell asleep.

Trinity woke up standing in the snow. She wore a white velvet cape. Her cape was long, and hung all the way to the ground. She was wearing a black corset dress, a taffeta skirt and bustle, full and elegant. She was confused why she was here and how she got here.

The wind circled around her. The landscape was white as far as the eye could see. She was alone. But she did not feel alone. She felt watched. The hairs on the back of her neck bristled. She looked around but could not see anyone.

She took one step in the snow and it crunched beneath her boots. She hiked her dress up out of the snow. She did not know which way to head. To the right she saw in the distance a grove of birch trees. She walked that direction. After a few steps she heard the crunch of footsteps behind her, like she was being followed. She stopped and turned but no one was there.

She continued walking toward the birch woods. Again she heard crunching behind her. She stopped suddenly and looked behind her. No one was there. She looked back in the snow and saw only her own footsteps.

Trinity was creeped out. She was nervous and on edge. The wind swirled around her and sounded as if it was calling her name.

"Trinity."

She looked around. Again she took several steps and she could hear the wind whispering her name.

She began to run toward the woods. She grabbed the front of her dress and ran as fast as she could through the snow, but her black combat boots could only take her so fast. Her dress dragged behind her in the snow. Her cape flew behind her waving in the wind, her hair whipping and lashing her face. She was nearing the edge of the grove. She looked behind her once more to see if anyone was following. But once again, she saw no one.

Just as she turned back toward the grove she nearly ran into Roan. He was dressed in black pants, black combat boots, and a ragged but formal-looking jacket with red and black military insignia on the jacket, like shoulder pads and patches. It was very grunge, almost gothic. He had chains hanging from his belt and his hair was spiked upward. It was as if they were both dressed up for something, but she did not know what.

She stood still, breathing heavily. She did not know what to do or say. She did not know if she should be scared or relieved to see another person.

He stared. She stared. The vapor of their breath hung heavy in the cold air. The standoff was tense.

He smirked. She took it as her cue to flee and bolted past him, running through the birch grove. She glanced behind her to see if he was following. He was still standing there, which frightened her more. It almost seemed like he was giving her a head start, just to make the game interesting. The terror drove her to run even faster.

Within seconds, Roan was chasing her. She ran harder and faster, occasionally glancing behind her. He chased her, his eyes cold, an evil smirk on his face. She did not know what he wanted or why she was running, except that he was bad news. If he was chasing her it was not a good thing.

Birch trees passed by in a blur. She jumped over roots and plants, her cape snagging behind her. But Roan was closing the gap. She knew she could not out run him. She knew she was going to need help.

Then she tripped when her dress caught on a root. She tugged at it desperately, the cold snow melting into her dress. Finally the dress tore and released her. She jumped to her feet and ran out of the woods and into an open field of snow.

She ran as fast as she could, but it was too late. Roan was right behind her. He grabbed her and threw her to the ground. She kicked and screamed and thrashed from side to side struggling to get away. Crawling on her hands and knees she scrambled to get away. He grabbed her ankle and dragged her to him, throwing her onto her back.

Suddenly Roan's face contorted and he grew a mouthful of sharp teeth. Before she knew what was happening Roan's teeth tore into her side. He chewed on her flesh. The pain was intense and she started to bleed out. She could see her own blood staining the white snow. Her body was cold and wet. She did not have the strength to push Roan off of her.

Within moments Roan had disappeared and she was left alone in the dimming light, lying in the snow, bleeding. She could not move. She only felt pain and cold. She was dying, lying there with snow flurries above her. She closed her eyes. Then everything went dark.

Trinity bolted awake. She was sweating, and yet cold and shivering. Her nightmare was intense and much too real. She still felt the pain and cold from her dream as she lay in bed suffering from the flu.

Just as she was about to get up to get something to drink, her brother came through the door. He carried a glass of Sprite. Nicholas sat on the edge of the bed and offered her the drink.

"The nurse says you are really sick."

"Flu."

"Yuck." He sat back a little. "Don't get me sick."

"I thought you liked to share everything. Come over here so I can wipe my sicko cooties on you."

They smiled at each other.

"I had a weird dream."

"About what?"

"Me and Roan. I was in a black ball gown and a white cape. I was out in the middle of a snow field and started running."

She recounted her dream, including the part where Roan grew sharp teeth and chewed off a chunk of her torso.

"Fangs like a vampire?" he asked.

"No, a mouthful of sharp, pointed, gruesome teeth."

Her brother frowned concerned. "It was just a dream. Relax. Logan and the others won't let anything bad happen to you."

Trinity sighed, not sure she was as immune from the Dark Ones as she hoped.

"Get some sleep so you can get well. I will bring you some soup at lunch," her twin offered.

Trinity snuggled down into her bed. She felt awful. And right now she felt vulnerable and weary from her dream. At least she hoped that's all it was...a dream.

Chapter Twenty-Five

Trinity awoke to a gentle knock on her bedroom door. At first she thought it was a part of her dream, but realized it was real.

"Come in," she said, weakly.

Logan came in with a breakfast tray. He had chicken noodle soup, fresh glass of Sprite and some toast.

"How are you feeling?" he asked.

Trinity shrugged.

"I hope you get better soon."

"So do I."

"I just thought maybe you were trying to get out of school for a while," Logan joked.

She groaned.

"I'd rather attend class than feel this crappy."

"You don't look so good," he said.

"How sweet of you," she said, swatting at him.

He blushed.

"I just mean that you are flushed, not that…"

"I know, I know, I'm just teasing."

Logan looked relieved to be off the hook.

"I talked to the nurse and she said it was just the flu and it will go away if you sleep it off."

"You talked to the nurse?" Trinity asked, curious.

"I just wanted to make sure you were going to be okay, that it wasn't anything serious."

Trinity thought that was sweet and teased him about it.

"Ah, you are worried about me," she crooned.

Logan blushed again.

"Of course I'm worried about you. I just want to find out how worried I need to be," he explained.

She smiled. He was too precious.

"You've been around a while and have seen all kinds of sickness. I get it," she said.

"You have no idea," he said smiling weakly.

She was not sure if she should tell him about her dream. Just as she decided to keep it to herself he asked her about it.

"Your brother said you had a pretty intense dream."

"It was just a dream," she said.

"Nicholas told me the entire dream. Roan killed you by biting you?" he asked.

"I know it sounds silly. But yes, he grew long sharp teeth and ripped my side to shreds and left me to die."

Logan looked perplexed.

"Should I be worried?" she half jested.

Logan was silent. That worried her.

"Last I looked Roan doesn't have teeth like that," she said.

Logan looked at her. She could not tell if he was concerned, or if he was hiding something from her.

"Don't worry about it. But make sure you tell me if you have any other dreams," he said.

"It's just a dream, right?" she asked.

"Most likely," he said tenderly. But she knew better. He was not giving her the whole truth.

"Just make wise choices, and be safe. Don't isolate yourself or let him corner you," he advised. "Your dream is probably your deepest fears manifesting themselves in a way that your brain can handle."

She understood that and hoped it was true.

"You should eat," he told her.

She sipped on a couple spoonfuls of soup and took a small bite of toast. She did not want to overdo it. Her stomach was weak and she was not sure how much it could handle. The last thing she wanted was to do was to puke all over Logan.

Logan changed the subject.

"We have plans that we want to talk to you and Nicholas about."

Trinity perked up. She had been waiting for the showdown.

"Once you are feeling better we can all sit down and talk."

"Why do we need to wait? We can talk now," she said.

Logan shook his head.

"We can wait. We will talk in a couple of days. Your health is important."

She was anxious. She did not want to be left out. He sensed her anxiety.

"Don't worry, we won't talk or make any plans without you," he assured her. "Trust me, we need your help."

She felt slightly better. She did not want to miss the action.

She leaned back and took another draw on the soup. She could not eat much more and asked him to take the tray. He placed the Sprite on her nightstand and removed the breakfast tray with the food. He offered to later come by and see her.

She needed her rest and was glad to lie back down and close her eyes. Just the short conversation had made her tired.

"Get some sleep," he said, as he brushed his hand over hers then headed out the door, closing it quietly behind him.

Trinity closed her eyes and went back to sleep, hoping not to meet Roan again in her dreams.

Chapter Twenty-Six

Trinity felt someone stroking her hand. She knew it was Logan and smiled.

"That's the first time you've enjoyed my touch," she heard a dark voice whisper.

Her eyes popped open. Roan sat on the side of her bed and had her hand in his. She pulled her hand back, disgusted. She stared at him fearful.

He grinned wickedly. I came to check on you.

"Whatever for? Now get out!" she said, forcefully.

"I heard you were sick and I just wanted to make sure it wasn't anything serious. We have a date later and I need you to be robust and healthy," he whispered in a sweet, cruel voice.

"We don't have a date!" she spat.

"Oh but yes we do and I think you've seen the outcome," he insisted.

She stared. He stared.

"Could he be talking about her dream?" she thought to herself.

She did not say a word.

He pressed, "You know what I am talking about it. You saw it. I saw it."

She sat silently, not willing to admit that he knew about her dream. Maybe someone had told him and he was messing with her. There is no way he knew without someone mentioning it. She needed to talk to her brother and Logan and find out who told Roan.

As if he knew what she was thinking he said, "I saw it too."

She shrugged. "What are you talking about?"

He grinned.

"Don't play games. We've never played games. It's one of the things I like about our relationship," he said.

"We don't have a relationship," she said, angrily.

"Don't change the subject," he said.

"You know what I know, and at some point in the future we have a date in the snow."

He blew her a kiss and left her room.

She shuddered. He terrified her.

A few minutes later Logan walked into her room.

The first words out of her mouth were, "Did you tell Roan about my dream or did he overhear you guys talking about it?"

Logan looked confused. "No. How would he have heard about it?"

"That's what I was wondering," she said.

"Did he know about your dream?" Logan asked, worried.

"Yes."

Logan looked frightened and peppered her with questions.

"How do you know that he knew? What did he know? When did you talk to him?"

Trinity told Logan that Roan was in her room earlier. She recounted their entire conversation. With each sentence Logan became more anxious. Finally, when she was finished telling him what happened, she had questions of her own.

"How did he know? What does that mean? Was it more than a dream?"

Logan placed her hand in his.

"Calm down. I'm sure he heard about it somewhere. You know how students love to spread these kinds of stories around." He tried to assure her, but she was not buying it.

"Logan don't sweet-talk me. I want the truth. Was this dream a premonition?" Trinity asked.

Logan looked at her. His eyes looked sad.

"Tell me the truth."

"I don't know Trinity. It could be a premonition or foreshadowing. It could be a dream. It hasn't happened yet which means it might not even happen. Life isn't predetermined. We make choices that lead us down different paths. You know that. We've talked about it regarding Cole."

Trinity was slightly relieved in a way. Even if it had been a premonition, Logan made a good point. It had not happened yet.

"I can't tell you too much. I'm not supposed to talk to you about the future even if I know something, which I don't. We can't see into the future. We simply react to life as you do."

He ran his hand down the side of her face.

"I will do everything in my power to protect you," he whispered.

She smiled.

"My own warrior angel," she said.

Logan leaned in a kissed her on the cheek.

"I'll be back in a little bit, I have a surprise." With that he left the room with a smile on his face. Trinity was curious what his surprise was.

Fifteen minutes later, Trinity heard voices outside her room. Her brother, Logan, Tristan, Alaina and Phoenix all crowded in. Logan wheeled in a television and a DVD player.

"We thought you could use a little company," Alaina said.

"Sorry we didn't invite any of your other friends, but they would all be susceptible to getting sick so we thought it best they stay away," Tristan said.

Logan put in the DVD and snuggled up on the bed with Trinity. Everyone else crowded onto the bed or pulled up chairs to watch the movie together.

Trinity was asleep before the movie ended. She never even heard everyone leave. Logan had even wheeled out the television without disturbing her.

Trinity woke up in the middle of the night with the cold shakes. She leaned over her bed and grabbed a sweatshirt. She noticed movement outside her window. She moved closer to the window in the dark, staying in the shadows.

She saw the four Dark Ones walking toward the woods and she wondered what they were up to. As if he sensed her watching him, Roan looked up at her. She gasped and shrunk back from the window, even though she knew he could not see her in the dark.

Tomorrow she would tell Logan about their midnight stroll. They were planning something and she needed to find out what it was.

Trinity lay back in bed with the covers pulled tightly to her chin. She could not fall back asleep. She knew that if she were not sick she would be out of her bed, knocking on her brother's door and they would be following the Dark Ones. That was how the twins found out everything else they knew about them. Trinity wondered if her brother saw them out his own window and was thinking the same thing. Maybe he was already out there. That idea worried her. She did not want him out there alone. She knew he would not be any safer if she was there, but the thought of their buddy system made things seem less dangerous.

Trinity contemplated wrapping up in a blanket and running down to her brother's room just to make sure he was there. Of course if she did that he would only wake up and escort her back to bed. So she snuggled in her covers. She strained to see out the window, looking for more movement. Eventually they would come back from wherever they went and a part of her wanted to see them return.

She could not keep her eyes open for very long and before she knew it she was fast asleep, her worry of where the Dark Ones had gone drifted away.

Chapter Twenty-Seven

When Trinity woke up in the morning she felt fine. The fever was gone, but when the nurse checked her out she advised staying out of school one more day. Trinity groaned. She did not want to stay in bed. But if the nurse did not give her the thumbs up, she could not return to class. So she decided to do a little reading on warrior angels or maybe snoop around to see if she could figure out what the Dark Ones were up to.

Her brother brought breakfast, which she ate while she sat alone in her bedroom. Boring. She took out the book that described warrior angels. She read about the Archangel Michael. He was apparently the head warrior angel. She read about how he fought in many wars mentioned in history. He is the most well-known angel.

She studied the drawings of the warrior angels. The tattoos on their bodies were exactly like she had seen on Logan. The designs were intricate, artistic and almost tribal. She read everything the book had on warrior angels. It went into detail about the different encounters mortals had with theses warrior. Several men told stories that they had seen warrior angels appear on battlefields with them.

The book described many different angels. Mortals had witnessed them in warrior attire with swords and other weapons. They have been seen in major battles throughout history, bare-chested with massive wings.

Trinity wondered how often humans had seen angels and not realized it. Logan, Tristan, Alaina and Phoenix could walk through the mall in their human form and no one would know the difference. Trinity felt special. She had a secret; not only had she seen angels, she was friends them. She blushed when she remembered she had a crush on one in particular, and he had kissed her. She could never reveal that Logan was an angel. Only her brother would know what he truly was.

She looked outside as a new snow flurry caught her attention. The school looked peaceful, but appearances were deceiving. There was a war waging on campus. Trinity shot up a little prayer. They all needed strength, wisdom and the ability to fight against the Dark Ones. As she prayed she realized Logan could probably hear her. The thought made her smile.

Trinity lay down for a nap, her eyes were tired and she didn't realize how exhausted one could get just from getting sick. The nurse told her she needed a day to recuperate. Her body had worked hard to fight off the virus.

As soon as she fell asleep, she found herself back in the snowy field. This time it was different. This time she was aware that it was a dream. She wore the same black corset dress and white cape. She saw the birch grove again to her right. Fear set in. She did not want to feel Roan tearing at her flesh again. She did not want to feel herself dying. She wondered if she ran another direction if she would escape the horrible fate at the end of this dream. Or would Roan just appear around that corner as well?

She decided to find out. She knew what would happen if she ran to the east so she ran west. The snow was endless without a building or tree in sight. But she ran anyway, hoping something would appear and she would find safety.

Her running soon became jogging, jogging became walking and walking became a trudge. Now the trudge grew difficult and her dress was soaked and dragged behind. Each step became heavier, but she was determined to keep moving. Without movement, hypothermia could set in. Step. Breath. Step. Breath. Step. Breath.

She realized she was hiking uphill and began to wonder if this had been the best idea. Just as she was considering turning back, she came to the crest of the hill and saw a village below. It was a quaint village in the English countryside, with cobblestone streets and stone buildings. She rushed down the hill toward the village. She had never been so happy to see civilization before. But one thing worried her. Where was Roan? Was he lurking nearby, ready to pounce? She was sure no human could battle against him alone.

By the time she reached the edge of the village is was dark. She ran to the first cottage and pounded on the door. No one answered. She ran to the next and pounded again begging for help. Again, silence. The entire town appeared absent of any life. Where was everyone? She ran down the cobblestone streets. A thick fog started to set in. The moon was full.

Trinity felt like the scene was set for a horror flick, where the damsel is about to be eaten by the big bad wolf. Just as she had that thought, her cape turned from white to crimson red. Trinity ran down one of the side streets, ripping off the cape as she went. She felt like an unwilling matador and she did not want the cape to bring the raging bull known as Roan.

She zigged and zagged down different streets, looking for signs of life. Windows were closed, doors were locked. Even the local pub was empty and dark. Picturesque street lamps provided only dim light, but only enough to illuminate the thickening fog.

She leaned against a light post to catch her breath. She realized she needed to hide in the shadows. She slipped down the side of another street and saw the red cape she had discarded. Was she running in circles? Worried, she backed away and began to run, as she ran her black dress turned the same deep crimson as the cape. Trinity groaned, sarcastically. If this was some ploy to take her dress off, it was not going to work. She would rather be a running target in a bull fight then escape naked!

Trinity was weary. She stopped running. She needed to conserve her energy. If no one was actually chasing her, then she needed to be calm and find someone to take her in. She could not stand out in the cold all night. She tried to open several doors but they were solid and would not budge. It was no use. No one was here.

She squatted down and leaned her head back against the wall of a stone building. The moon shown down on the river running through the village. The setting was quite beautiful, depressing, but beautiful. She closed her eyes and tried to wake up. She could not wake from her dream.

"At least I'm not dead," she thought to herself.

"Not yet," she heard a voice from several yards away.

She looked up and there was Roan, dressed as he had been in her other dream. She remained still, squatting and staring up at him. She did not know if she could get up and run. She was tired, wet and there was no way she was going to outrun him. He was within striking distance of her right now anyway.

"You going to run?" he asked, curious.

"Debating on it," she replied, exhausted.

His eyebrows arched, amused.

"I'll give you a head start."

She sighed and gave him an I'm-not-amused look.

"What fun is it if there is no chase?" he sneered.

"Eat me," she said, defiantly extended her bare arm to offer him a bite.

He stared. She stood.

169

"Here I am, big boy."

Outwardly she stood strong, defiant. But inside she was praying. Praying that Logan would come, praying that any help would come. Praying that they would have the right weapons to defeat Roan. Praying for her protection and that she would live.

Roan skulked closer. His human teeth were still intact, that was a good sign. That meant she at least had a few more seconds to live.

"I've not known you to be a quitter," he said, confused.

"I'm not. But I'm also realistic. And my chances of running from you and escaping are slim to none."

"You are weak," he mocked.

"Possibly," she said, with no remorse.

Her strategy was to burn time while she prayed and hoped that Logan or one of the other angels might appear.

Logan had told her of the story of Daniel, who had prayed for an angel. The angel had been dispatched, but was delayed for two weeks fighting the Prince of Persia, a powerful demon. She certainly hoped it would not take an angel two weeks to respond, because she would be dead within a few minutes. But buying more time, however, just might save her life.

"Run!" he screamed at her.

She refused. Roan snarled. He stepped in closer, inches from her face. He placed his hands on her waist. Trinity noted that his hands were placed were placed exactly where he had bitten her last time.

"I'm not afraid of you," she told him quietly.

"You will be when you see what I really look like," he snarled.

"I've seen."

The silence between the two of them filled her ears. Roan was mystified by this girl. He had never met anyone like her. She was immune to his touch and she was not afraid of him; even though she knew what he looked like and that knew that he could tear her to pieces in a matter of seconds.

She was not weak. She was strong and intelligent. It made him want to corrupt her even more. To make her want him, to make her need him, to make her weak and unable to resist temptation.

"He doesn't love you," Roan said, changing his tactic.

"He doesn't have too," she replied, calmly.

"You are just a pawn in his game. He is using you."

"I'm okay with that."

"Why? Why not come with me, switch to my side. I won't use you. I will give you power," he crooned seductively.

"I would rather be a pawn and used to further what is good and right, than be the Queen of Evil."

Roan could not crack her. He could not tempt her. He kept his hands on her waist. He brushed his cheek against hers and inhaled her sent.

"T...R...I...N...I...T...Y," he whispered in her ear with hot breath.

They brushed noses. He exhaled and whispered her name again.

She stood there, cold and alert. He pressed his body against hers and smelled her hair.

"You smell delicious."

"You smell like wet dog."

He chuckled. He cupped her chin in his palm.

"I know what Logan sees in you."

Silence. He searched her eyes. Then once again brushed his cheek against hers.

"Join me," he begged.

"Never!"

He was frustrated. He took a few steps back to contemplate his next move. If he had been Zoenn, his anger would have gotten the best of him. But anger was not his weakness.

He jumped into her, pushing her roughly back against the wall. Her skull smacked against the stone, but she remained conscious. She stood there, without fighting, staring at him. He grabbed her hair and tilted her head to one side.

"I am going to tear your head off! I am going to gnaw through your neck, until your head is severed from your shoulders."

Trinity prayed harder. This was the moment she needed help. This was the moment she needed to be saved. She had stalled as long as she could, longer than she would have been able to run had she fled.

Roan's sharp teeth appeared. This was it. Trinity was going to die, again. Then, just as he lunged at her neck, a sword thrust between her neck and Roan's teeth. Roan leapt away, fearful of the sword. Logan was here! He stood with the tip of his sword pointed

172

toward Roan and stepped between the two of them to shield Trinity. Roan sharp teeth and demonic visage morphed back to human form.

There was a tense moment, each immortal sizing up the other. Trinity wondered if Roan was contemplating whether he should fight or retreat.

"Leave her alone," Logan said, calmly.

"How did you know to come?" Roan asked.

"She asked me to."

"She prayed?"

Logan nodded. Roan looked over to Trinity.

"She's discovered her power," Logan smirked.

Roan was disgusted. He backed off a few steps.

Pointing at Trinity, "This isn't over."

Then he vanished.

Logan put his sword away and turned to Trinity.

"Power?" Trinity asked.

"Prayer."

Trinity hugged Logan. She was glad that he had come. She knew this was just a dream, but he had come, and had changed the ending of her dream.

"We need to get back," he said as he grabbed her hand they ran down the foggy cobblestone streets of the deserted village. Her vision became hazy. Within seconds Trinity woke up and found herself in her own bedroom, lying on the bed, exhausted.

She sat up and pondered her latest dream. She remembered what Logan had told her; though her dreams foreshadowed future events, those events could change. The next time, no matter what kind of pickle she got herself into, she was going to pray for help.

Nicholas knocked on her door and walked in carrying lunch. Trinity was famished. She did not feel tired anymore and she was not sick. She was itching to get out of her room.

She told him about her brother about her dream. Nicholas liked this one better since his sister did not get torn apart like a chew toy. But he still did not like that it was a close call. Nicholas gave his sister a hug to comfort her and told her to hang in there. The nurse had assured her that by dinner time she would be well enough to good to go back to civilization. She would be released from her cage tonight.

Trinity rehearsed her dream several times, thinking through the different elements. She decided that should she have the same dream again she would run a different direction. She also wondered what would happen if she ran back to the birch tree woods but prayed for help this time. Trinity did not know how many times she was going to have this dream, but she wanted to explore all her options, to prepare her for the time it all became real.

Later, while Trinity was catching up on homework for the classes she missed, Roan walked into her room. He did not knock. He just walked in like it was his room.

"Get. Out." Trinity said.

He ignored her and walked to the bed. He leaned over the bed leering at her with his dark and cold eyes.

"This doesn't change anything," was all he said.

"Change what?" she asked, innocently. But she knew full well that Roan actively and consciously took part in her dreams. It was becoming clear to Trinity that it was more than a dream; it was more like a spiritual realm. A very real, but spiritual, realm.

He leaned closer to her, inches from her face. She stared at him, not backing down.

"It is a shame that such a passionate intellect is going to waste. You could do great things for us." With that he backed away and walked out the door.

Trinity wanted to yell after him that she planned to use her "passionate intellect" to do great things, just not his great things.

Roan was evil. His cause included the slaughter and murder of innocent men, women and children. Their plans involved the destruction of lives, families, and nations. Why would Roan think she wanted to be a part of any of that?

Chapter Twenty-Eight

The next morning Trinity woke up and was ready to get back to school. Lying around in bed for a couple days was a nice break, but she could do without the sick. She dressed in a red and black plaid skirt and grabbed her black leather jacket and red scarf. She tromped out through the snow to the dining hall. Nicholas ran up beside her.

"You're looking better."

"You implying I looked awful yesterday?"

"Yup!"

"Gee thanks!"

"I just tell it like it is, sis."

Smiles from both.

When they entered the dining hall, all Trinity's friends were glad to see her well. Logan put his arms around her and gave her a big bear hug of relief.

As they sat down he leaned over.

"After breakfast, we need to talk with you and Nicholas."

Trinity was intrigued. They had a plan. She could barely eat. She was nervous and excited. Everyone else seemed calm and went about breakfast like normal. Trinity was glad to be back. She did not realize how much she missed the friendly breakfast banter.

Later Trinity and Nicholas went with the new kids to their spot out in the birch grove. They could not risk anyone seeing them or overhearing what they had to talk about.

Tristan began.

"We need to have a private meeting with Cole; sometime when the dark ones cannot interrupt and try to influence him."

"We have decided to do it on Christmas Eve," Alaina said.

"What is significant about Christmas Eve?" Trinity asked.

"Christmas Eve is one of the most powerful nights of the year," Logan explained.

"It is the night that goodness came into the world as a baby. That makes it the most special night of the year. Nothing like it had ever happened before and nothing like it has happened since," Phoenix explained.

Nicholas and Trinity understood. The special phenomenon in history made that night memorable and historical.

"We are going to send Cole an invite to meet with us at midnight on Christmas Eve, in the cathedral. The hour before we

177

meet with him we will all get together and perform a sacred ritual to prepare for the intervention," Logan said.

"Then we will confront him and try to release him from the bonds of the Dark Ones, Alaina said. "Hopefully he will respond well and be able to make a wise decision for himself,"

"Tell us where and when you need us and we will be there to help," Nicholas said.

"Meet us Christmas Eve, in the cathedral, at 11pm," Tristan told them. "We will take care of everything else."

They nodded. The meeting was adjourned. Carefully they all returned to class. Trinity tried not to draw attention to herself when she walked into class late.

Christmas was two weeks away. There was the annual talent performance here at the school and she still needed to do her Christmas shopping. They had one more day of school and then they were on Christmas break. She was looking forward to the free time. She wanted to spend more time with Logan.

Trinity tried to get through her day without any problems from the Dark Ones. It seemed even the Dark Ones had something else on their minds, because they did not harass Trinity. At lunch the day was still uneventful. Trinity, her brother and the new kids talked and joked. The conversation buzzed about Christmas break.

"Trinity, are you going to perform for the talent show?" Riley asked.

Trinity shrugged.

"What's your talent?" Logan asked, curious.

Trinity shrugged.

"Please don't tell me you twirl a baton to marching band music," Tristan joked.

Trinity shrugged.

"She's a songwriter and she sings," Nicholas blurted.

"Yes, she's gonna perform in the show," Anthony insisted. "Otherwise I've been learning her new song for nothing."

"What do you play?" Alaina asked Anthony.

"He is amazing on the drums," Riley said, smiling shyly at Anthony.

Trinity grinned, knowing Riley would sing Anthony's praises all day long. Riley still had a major crush on the techie geek.

"You have a band?" Logan asked.

"Something like that," Trinity said.

"I can't wait to see you perform!" Logan said.

Trinity felt her face flush and she did not know what to say. Luckily she did not have to, lunch was over and everyone scurried off to their next class. She barely stayed awake through history class, as her professor drone on about the French Revolution. Usually she enjoyed this class, but today all she could think about was Christmas break, shopping and the new plans she had for late Christmas Eve.

She made it to her last class where she was encompassed by Logan and all the others. There was a buzz in the room. No one could pay attention or focus. The professor finally gave up and assigned some homework for the break and then dismissed everyone. Everyone cheered.

Trinity and Logan walked out of the classroom together. He helped her gather all her books from her locker. Students were whooping and hollering throughout the halls.

Once outside and headed toward the dorms, Logan asked, "So why aren't you guys going home for Christmas this year?"

"Normally we do, and we have all the family over. It's the best time of year," Trinity said. "But this year, our parents…" she did not know if she could finish the sentence.

"Something wrong?" Logan asked.

"Oh no, I just don't know how much I am allowed to talk about. But you are not exactly human, so it might be ok," she answered.

Nicholas showed up just at that moment.

"What aren't you allowed to talk about?"

"Mom and dad's job."

Nicholas thought about it for second, then answered, "It's probably ok to tell him. I don't think he can compromise their position."

Trinity looked from her brother to Logan and then back to her brother again.

Nicholas shrugged and said, "Our parents work for the United States government. We aren't even supposed to know, but we found out a couple years ago."

Logan nodded, understanding.

Trinity said, "This Christmas they are…somewhere else."

"They travel a lot?" Logan asked.

Trinity nodded, "That is why we are here at Shadowland."

180

"They only missed one other Christmas when we were kids. We ended up staying with our grandparents and celebrated with aunts and uncles and cousins," Nicholas explained.

"So why don't you go celebrate with your grandparents this year?" Logan asked.

Trinity and Nicholas looked at each other, then back at Logan.

"They asked us if we wanted to, but we told them we wanted to stay here," Trinity offered.

Logan smiled. He knew it had something to do with him and that made him happy. He'd never had these feelings before. Angels were not supposed to fall in love with mortals.

"Is Cole not going home for Christmas?" Trinity asked, wondering if they had thought their plan through.

"No. He told his parents he didn't want to go home," Logan said.

"Must be hard when your parents are going through a divorce," Trinity said, sympathetically.

"So what does everyone that stays here do on Christmas break?" Logan asked.

"No one will go home until after the talent performance, which is tomorrow night," Trinity explained. "Then about two-thirds the kids go home and the rest stay. The school plans a trip to London so we can all go Christmas shopping and have a little break."

"We've never been here over Christmas break so I don't really know what to expect," Nicholas said.

They all agreed to put their books and away and meet in the commons room. They spent the rest of the afternoon playing games with other students and watching Christmas movies. Everyone was ready for a break from school.

When dinner was ready everyone walked over to the dining hall. For the first time, Trinity realized she had not seen the Dark Ones all day. They were not in classes, or around anywhere. She leaned over and asked Logan, "Where are they?"

Logan shrugged.

"They are up to something. We just don't know what."

The thought sent chills up Trinity's spine. She did not like not knowing where they were. It frightened her a little, especially since she started having the dreams.

When they entered the dining hall Trinity noticed Sabrina and Cole at the Dark Ones' table with their friends, but the Dark Ones were missing.

Just after the food was served a cold draft drifted through the dining room. Trinity had the chills. She knew something was wrong and looked around to see what it was. She noticed Logan and the others were also aware and on guard. Then the Dark Ones entered the dining room together. The room hushed a little. The Dark Ones fed on their fear.

Roan looked at Trinity and blew her a kiss. She did not flinch. She watched them walk to their table and sit down with Cole. The dining hall grew noisy again as everyone resumed their banter.

Trinity was curious.

"When they leave like that and return suddenly, where did they go?"

Logan looked at her and did not know how much to tell her. He did not know how much she could comprehend.

"What? Are they going to hell and back?" she joked.

"Not really," Logan answered, smiling. "They are going to another....," he didn't know how to finish.

"Dimension, realm, somewhere mortals can't see?" she asked.

"Something like that."

She surprised him and said playfully, "I get it. There is another dimension where you spiritual species hang out and we mortals aren't invited."

Logan smiled. Everyone finished their dinner and decided to turn in early for the night. Trinity was exhausted.

As she got ready for bed, she looked out her window at the winterscape and breathed a little prayer, "Help us. Help Cole. Help us help Cole."

Then she laughed at her sophomoric prayer. But this time, she knew someone out there was listening.

Chapter Twenty-Nine

The outdoor amphitheater was full. All the students and faculty had gathered for the annual talent performance underneath the starry night. It was not snowing, which made it nice. But everything was covered in snow making the setting feel magical.

The school had outdoor heaters which filled the amphitheater and made it toasty warm. There was an elaborate lighting and sound system for the stage.

Trinity stood backstage, waiting for her turn. She was last. She wore a white dress with a tulle skirt that was full to the knees. A black satin ribbon tied around her waist and bowed in the back. As usual she sported her combat boots and black and white striped thigh-high socks with her dress. Her hair loosely hung down her back and her eyes sparkled. She licked her cherry red lips nervously.

The stage was lighted with hundreds of white candles. Soft and charming. Perfect.

The stage director told Trinity it was her turn. She walked out to the center of the stage behind the microphone. The crowd was silent with anticipation. The pianist began the simple, haunting accompaniment. Trinity's pure voice rang out. The gothic melody in A-minor captivated the audience. When she got to the chorus, she played her red electric guitar, Anthony joined with the drums and the bass guitar started thumping. They rocked.

The crowd loved every note of it. Everything about the performance was "Trinity". This was her essence, her soul and she was baring it to everyone.

On the last chorus it began to snow. The flurries came down and each snowflake was illuminated by candlelight. The moment was magical.

When Trinity sang her last note, the crowd erupted with cheers and applause. Trinity shyly nodded to the crowd and exited the stage. She was excited and happy. She loved performing and sharing her art. Her moment in the spotlight had been perfect.

Her brother ran up and gave her a big hug.

"You were amazing!" he whispered.

She smiled and hugged him back. Logan came up and gave Trinity a hug as well.

"I am speechless," was all he could utter. "You have a special gift."

Trinity was glowing. This had been a star-filled night for her.

Chapter Thirty

Today the students who remained at the school for the holidays got to go into London for an overnighter to Christmas shop and have a little fun. Trinity packed her bag and bundled up for the winter weather.

When she met up with her brother and Logan in the downstairs hall, everyone was ready to go.

"I've never done anything like this before," Logan said.

"We've never been so intertwined with humans like this. This entire plan is different," Tristan said.

Trinity did not know if Tristan was upset about the idea that a couple mortals were going to help or how she was supposed to take his comment.

Alaina jumped in and explained.

"Normally we keep to ourselves and don't interact with humans that much. But this is different since you have figured out who we are and who the Dark Ones are."

"There is a purpose for it," Phoenix said.

"I've never bought a Christmas present before," Logan said, smiling.

Trinity grinned at Logan. He was a little kid on his first field trip. She took his hand and they all got on the bus to go to the train station. The train ride into London would take about an hour.

Once on the train Trinity, who was sitting by the window, settled in and enjoyed the passing scenery. She was excited and happy. She loved London at Christmas time. All the stores were lit up with twinkle lights. There were carolers in the streets. The shops had fun and unique items to purchase. The local pubs and restaurants were bubbly and filled the night with merriment. Plus, the theater district near Soho was spectacular. You could find whatever play or musical you wanted to see. Trinity and Logan talked the entire train ride.

When they arrived in London, the group of students and their chaperones checked into the hotel which was situated in Covent Garden. Nicholas and Trinity loved the neighborhood. All the junior and senior students were given a map and told what time to be back in the evening. The freshmen and sophomore students all had chaperones. There were basic rules for the juniors and seniors. No walking around alone and stay in groups of three or more.

Trinity, her brother and the four others made up a group of six so they were covered.

They all wanted to check out the neighborhood. Of course Logan and the others had seen London a gazillion times considering they had been alive since before its existence. But Logan said that he had never seen it like this before, from a human perspective.

"I've never had anyone to buy a gift for," he said.

Trinity thought about this and wondered how she was going to buy him a gift. After all, what do you get for the immortal that has everything?

As if reading her thoughts, he said, "Your friendship is the best gift I could ever get."

Trinity felt the same. But she knew she was young and she had her entire life ahead of her. It was entirely possible Logan would be gone in a few months. She did not want to get too attached. It was just a high school crush, was it not? But for some reason, deep down, she felt it might be more.

She felt like Juliet in Shakespeare's play. She was in love with a Romeo and the two of them could never be together. Their love was forbidden. Star-crossed.

Trinity snapped back to reality.

"I'm starving!" her brother announced.

The group agreed and they plodded off to find something to eat. They finally agreed on a little Indian restaurant off Piccadilly. Trinity found English food to be very bland and the best she could hope for was that an Indian restaurant would add a little spice and flavor to the food.

Over lunch Nicholas and Trinity put together a game plan. They needed to buy gifts for their parents, but they also needed to buy gifts for each other. Trinity wanted to buy Logan something, even though he did not need anything. They decided to stay together for a while and then separate with Trinity, Alaina and Tristan headed in one direction and Logan, Phoenix and Nicholas headed in another. Then they would all meet up at the hotel at the designated time to get ready for dinner and their evening out.

It took Nicholas and Trinity quite some time to find a gift for their parents. The group stopped and bought a snack and decided to split up. Trinity was sad to part with Logan, but she needed to buy him and her brother a gift.

Tristan, Alaina and Trinity walked in a different direction than the other group. Alaina hooked her arm through Trinity's red wool coat.

"What are you going to get Logan?" she asked.

"I don't even know where to start," she answered. "He can't keep anything really, can he?"

Alaina shrugged.

"I don't know, we've never tried before."

The three of them walked in silence a block or two peering in shop windows. Tristan broke the silence.

"This doesn't happen often you know."

"A mortal buying an immortal a gift?" Trinity asked.

"No. A human and an angel falling for each other."

"Has it been done before?" she asked.

"At one point, angels took humans as wives and they had children. The entire story was documented in scripture, but it's all a little cryptic."

"What do you think about it?" Trinity asked.

Silence.

"I don't know what I think about it," he finally answered.

"Is there a possible happy ending?" she asked.

He shrugged.

"Do you feel?" she asked.

Tristan smiled.

"We feel, we are happy, we are sad, we have all the emotions that you were created with. We even love, but we were made to love our Creator. It's the idea of an angel falling in love with another being that gets sketchy."

"Obviously you were created with the ability because it has happened," Trinity said.

"You may be right," Tristan mused.

"Definitely a gray area," said Alaina.

"But there is still the unanswered question of how would it ever work?" Trinity asked.

"There is that," Tristan said.

No one had the answer so they left it at that.

Trinity decided she was going to enjoy every moment she had with Logan and not worry about the future. If it came time to say goodbye she would deal with it then.

The three of them had fun poking in and out of shops. Alaina and Trinity tried on some clothes. Trinity found a black, knee length trench coat that laced up red in the back and had a very European collar. She loved it and just had to buy it. London had such fun fashion and everything was stylish and modern. Tristan just rolled his eyes every time the girls oohed and aahed over something.

"Alaina you may be immortal, but you're still a girl," he remarked.

The girls laughed. They then made Tristan try on a very gothic-looking top hat with black and red striped ribbon around it and a chain hooked to a pendant.

Trinity grabbed Tristan's head and pulled it down so she could get a better look at the pendant on the hat.

She laughed out loud.

"How fitting! You are totally buying that hat for the masquerade ball."

Alaina grabbed Tristan's head and looked at the pendant. She smiled, took the hat off and turned it around so Tristan could see. It was angel wings.

They bought the hat and Alaina and Trinity looked around the store for some more angel wing items. Trinity found another pendant with a few chains hanging from it stringing out to a black safety pin. She bought it to wear on her dress to the masquerade ball.

They had a lot of fun shopping, but Trinity still had not found anything unique to get Logan. She bought her brother a couple small things and then found a series of books she knew he would love. She decided she would have to go out again tomorrow. Right now they needed to get back to the hotel.

Back at the hotel, they went to their rooms to get ready for dinner. All the students and chaperones were going to dinner and then to see a musical. Trinity washed off and dressed for a night out. She raced back down to the lobby and found all her friends already waiting. Everyone was bundled with hats, scarfs and wool coats. December in London was blustery and cold.

When they stepped outside their hotel, the sky was dark and starry. But the streets were alive and bright. There were colorful Christmas lights and small, white twinkle lights. Each shop window had a Christmas theme. Carolers stood outside the hotel and sang "Angels we have heard on high." Trinity smiled at Logan.

When the carolers sang the line, "Sweetly singing o'er the plane," Logan leaned over and whispered to Trinity, "You're the one that sings sweetly."

She gave him a silly grin.

"Ah, that was sweet, but cheesy."

"Ouch," he retorted.

"You're the one that sings sweetly," she mocked him.

"Ok, yes…cheesy," he admitted. "But it's true I've never heard any angel sing like you do."

"I can live with that," Trinity said smugly.

Logan chuckled. He looked down at her hands. He wanted to hold her hand. But this was a school outing and it was forbidden.

"I'm wearing mittens," she said knowing what he was thinking.

He smiled.

"You sure you're not a mind reader?" he asked.

"Maybe just my brother's sometimes," she said.

"The twin thing."

"Can you explain it? Is there something about twins? I've heard about twins being separated at birth and when they find each other they are so similar it's scary." Trinity wanted answers.

"You began life at the same time, formed from the same genes. In the womb your brain, heart and consciousness began to form, grow and function. You spent nine months together in your mother's womb, experiencing the same things. There is just something special about twins." Logan tried to explain.

"Yes, but the ability to know what each other is thinking, even when we aren't in the same room?" she asked.

"It's a psychological connection starting from the moment you were conceived."

"Is it ESP or a psychic connection?" she asked.

"Humans have tried to explain and categorize oddities like twins' connection for centuries. I don't want to place your connection with your brother into one of those boxes. But know that you have an ability that is unique to twins, and not all twins have it."

"I think I can understand most of what you are saying," she said.

"Twins are special. Different. A unique phenomenon. Each created purposefully." he said.

"I agree with that statement. And considering these twins are walking down the sidewalk with a group of angels I'd say we are pretty special," Trinity joked.

The two exchanged a smile.

"What's amazing to me is here you are walking down the street in London on a December evening and all these people walking by don't even know they are in the presence of an immortal, another species, another supernatural being," Trinity said amazed.

Logan looked at her with a wry grin.

"What?" she asked.

"It happens all the time."

"With you?"

"With all of us."

"With all the angels in the world?"

"Angels walk among you every day and no one knows."

Trinity smiled and the two walked side by side until they reached the restaurant. Logan opened the door for her and they went inside with the other students. Everyone sat down to a nice dinner. Since there were extra ears they kept to neutral subject matters. No talk about the Dark Ones, or their plan on Christmas Eve.

It was a nice change. Everyone talked about Christmas, the snow and being in London. It was like a scene from a movie. Looking through the window from the snowy sidewalk, a group of friends, dressed festively for the holidays, breaking bread and laughing.

No one would guess they were entertaining angels unaware.

Chapter Thirty-One

Inside the theater all the students waited in anticipation as the curtain rose. They were here to see the classic musical, "White Christmas". As the music soared and the opening act began, Trinity slipped her hand into Logan's. He gave her a sideways smile and the two enjoyed their first holiday evening together.

On the way home from the theater all the students linked arms and sang Christmas carols as they tromped through the snow back to their hotel.

Trinity felt normal today. This was a good thing.

"It was nice to do fun, human activities," she thought. The last month or so she had been watching demons take over her school, hanging out with an angel and trying to battle strange and dangerous oddities. Tonight, she was just a teenage girl, hanging with her friends.

Once back at the hotel everyone hated to part ways. Trinity did not want to lose sight of Logan. Today had been one of the best days of her life. She was afraid that if she went to sleep, tomorrow she would wake up and it would all have been just a dream. She kept reminding herself that someday it would all be over, that she should just enjoy each second that she had.

Everyone headed off to their bedrooms. The plan was to meet again tomorrow for more shopping and a visit to the National Gallery, before heading home. Trinity and Logan stayed behind while everyone went to their rooms. Logan pulled her to the side of the lobby. There was a large Christmas tree, a fire in the white mantled fireplace and plush velvet seating. Once out of view of the others, he pulled her close and leaned over her.

"It would just be wrong if I didn't honor your traditions," he whispered.

She looked at him quizzically. He looked up. Her eyes followed his, and there, hanging above them, was a little twisp of mistletoe.

"I believe in tradition," she said.

He leaned in and kissed her tenderly. He was warm and she was filled with peace and happiness. Besides seeing her parents always come home safe from an assignment, kissing Logan was the most wonderful feeling she had ever experienced.

Quickly he released her and the two ran off to their separate rooms.

Chapter Thirty-two

Trinity was ready and waiting downstairs before anyone else the next morning. She still needed to find Logan a gift. But instead of separating from him half the day she decided she would hang out with everyone. When she saw something she wanted to get him, Alaina would distract him and Trinity would buy the gift.

They all went to see some of the tourist sites like Big Ben and Westminster Abbey. The sun was bright and glistened off the snow. Logan did not leave Trinity's side.

"I wish you could tell me about some of your adventures," she said, wistfully.

"I will someday," he said.

"There's got to be one adventure you can tell me about that wouldn't cause some major catastrophe if I knew," she said.

"There are a few, yes. Not everything I do is life-altering or world-changing," he said, grinning.

"So tell me about one," she persisted.

Logan looked off into the distance.

"Okay, there was one time that an old man was having trouble with kids break into his house. He was getting tired of it and there wasn't anything the police could do unless they caught them in the act." Logan began his story, slightly excited that he could share with her.

"Don't get excited. This is just a small side story I'm telling you about."

"I'll take whatever I can get. Even if you saved an ant, I'm excited to hear it," she teased.

"So, we were in route headed from one assignment to the next and this old guy sends up a little prayer for help just as the kids arrived to rob his house again. Apparently they had brought friends and the old guy was nervous about being outnumbered. We took a little detour, and stopped to help."

"What did you do?" Trinity asked.

"We showed up standing behind the old man when the kids came into the front yard with their hammers and baseball bats."

"If you were outnumbered, how did you scare off the troublemakers?"

"We just appeared, standing behind the old man," said Logan, with a smile. Then he leaned in. "Not in human form."

Trinity looked, wide-eyed.

"You appeared as angels, wings and all?"

"Well, something like that. But yes, we were in full armor and ready for battle. The kids took one look at us and freaked out. The funny part was, the old man thought it was him and his golf club that scarred the troublemakers off. He was hollering after them, 'there will be more of this if you ever come back here!'"

Trinity laughed. She could just imagine.

"Did the old man ever see you guys?"

"Nope. We took off before he even turned around."

"Just a fun little detour, huh?" She laughed.

Logan shrugged. "Perks of the job."

The two continued to share adventures, when Trinity noticed a little shop and something in the window. It was at that moment that she knew what she wanted to get Logan for Christmas. But in order to purchase it, she needed to be alone. She tried to think through how to go about it and then came up with an idea. She was going to have to break some rules.

She pulled her brother aside and told him she needed to be alone for an hour. He did not like the secrecy but his sister was stubborn and she would find a way with or without his help. So he covered for her while she ran back to the little shop to buy her Christmas present. It was really as much a present for herself as it was for Logan, but she knew it was what she wanted to do.

Once she had purchased it she hid it carefully and rejoined the other students to visit the National Gallery. The students poured from room to room viewing the paintings. One painting caught Trinity's eye and she sat down on the bench to absorb it.

Everyone else moved on and she was left by herself. She could not stop looking at the painting. Her eyes moved over every inch, taking in the colors, textures and content.

After twenty minutes Logan came looking for her. He sat down next to her and stared at the painting that had captivated her attention.

"What do you like about this one?" he asked, intrigued.

"Look closely" she said, not taking her eyes off the painting.

Logan stood up, walked close to the painting and searched. He got a funny look on his face, turned and looked at Trinity.

"What do you see?" he asked.

She stood, walked to him and the painting.

"You."

Both turned to look at the painting closely and sure enough there was a scene of men being protected by angels. There were four angels guarding the men. Logan, Tristan, Phoenix and Alaina.

"You want to explain?" Trinity said grinning.

Logan grinned back sheepishly.

"Not while standing next to my portrait."

The two moved away from the painting into another room.

"That painting was made in the 1700's," Trinity said.

"Well apparently that artist was so inspired by what he saw that he decided to immortalize the moment," said Logan.

"So, it really was you guys and that painting really did happen?" she asked.

"Yup."

Trinity smiled.

"You weren't expecting to see a painting of yourself were you?"

"Nope."

"Maybe we should get out of here before anyone else notices the similarities," she suggested.

"Yup."

"Got anything else to say?"

"Nope."

The two smiled and left the museum.

Chapter Thirty-Three

After they had toured the museum the group ate lunch at a cute little pub near Leicester Square. Everyone had most of their shopping done and now they were sight-seeing.

As they ate lunch a group of carolers came by and sung Christmas carols to the patrons in the pub. The carolers were dressed in old-fashioned, Victorian clothes. Their dresses swished in the snow and their hands were tucked in their fur muffs. Logan held Trinity's hand. Trinity savored the moment. They were creating a memory, a warm fuzzy she would always remember.

While they strolled down the street, back towards the hotel to check out, Trinity was quiet. Logan kept glancing at her trying to figure out what she was thinking. Finally he just asked.

"What are you thinking about?"

"What, you can't read my mind?" she teased.

"I think we've established I can't."

She smiled, then fell silent.

"So?" he asked.

"What?"

"Thoughts?"

"Oh yeah," she said, and smiled sheepishly. "I was just thinking about that painting."

Another pause.

"I was wondering, if there were others? There are so many paintings with angels in them. Are those real angels as well or just an artist's imagination?"

"All of the above," Logan answered.

"Ya, that's what I was thinking."

"Well?"

"I think I want that painting," she said with a wry grin.

Surprised.

"Really?"

"Then when you're gone, I'll always have it and remember that this chapter in my life wasn't just a dream."

Logan was amused.

"That painting is in a private collection, on loan to the museum. It's probably worth millions."

"I know," she shrugged. "Someday."

He smiled.

As they passed over the Westminster Bridge, Logan grabbed her hand and pulled her down the street.

"I have an idea!"

The two went running down the street as the rest of the group lagged behind. Logan slowed down when they came to a couple artists on the side of the road painting the London landscape.

"Would you paint us?" Logan asked one of the artists with paintings displayed for sale.

"Of course," the artist said, as he began to sketch a portrait of Logan and Trinity with London in the background.

Trinity was tickled Logan had thought of this idea. It was brilliant and risky at the same time. It probably was not a good idea for Logan to willingly immortalize himself in art, but she appreciated that he was doing it for her. For the duration of the sitting he had his arms wrapped around her as they posed happily for the artist.

When they were done Logan paid the artist, who wrapped and bagged her painting. Trinity smiled up at Logan.

"Thank you."

"You're welcome."

"This was a big deal, I know."

He shrugged, knowing it was.

They found the others in a souvenir shop nearby. They grabbed a cab and went back to the hotel. They checked out with the rest of their classmates and boarded the train to go back to Shadowland Academy.

This had been a wonderful trip. It was a respite from the drama of their lives the past few months. Trinity knew she would remember it the rest of her life.

Once back at school, the new kids told Trinity and Nicholas that they would send Cole the letter the following day. They had two days until Christmas Eve and they needed to prepare for the event. This was their opportunity to make history, to help Cole change his life path.

Logan reminded Trinity that one of the best things she could do to prepare was to use her power. Specifically to pray that Cole's heart would be prepared.

As she headed to bed that night she prayed just that.

Chapter Thirty-Four

The next day everyone ate a late breakfast. Tristan told them he had invited Cole to meet with them on Christmas Eve. They did not know if he would come or not, but they were prepared.

The plan was to spend an hour beforehand preparing, then at midnight on Christmas Eve they would make an appeal Cole. They would explain to him what was ahead of him. It was still his choice and they could not force him to make any decisions. But this was an opportunity on a very special night to isolate Cole from the demons and give him a chance to make a decision free of their influence.

Everyone spent the day wrapping presents and watching Christmas movies. Trinity kept her gift to Logan hidden. The group watched every Christmas movie they could get their hands on; all the Santa Claus movies, Deck the Halls, White Christmas, National Lampoons Christmas, Christmas in Connecticut, The Christmas Story, and several more. By the end of the day everyone was sugared out from all the candy canes and excited about Christmas Eve.

The night before Christmas Eve everyone sat in the commons room with the lights off, except the lights on the Christmas tree. Trinity sat on the couch with Logan. She melted into his side, his arm around her. Bing Crosby crooned in the background, Christmas presents were nestled under the tree. No one spoke. Everyone simply soaked in the Christmas spirit.

The next morning everyone woke up, slumped on the coach and some in lazy chairs. The tree was still lit, the morning light poured through the windows. The snow outside looked cold and in contrast made the room feel cozy. Everyone stretched and slowly began to get up. Logan smiled down at Trinity snuggled in the crook of his arm.

"Merry Christmas Eve," he whispered.

"Merry Christmas Eve."

Everyone just lay around for a few minutes trying to wake up. Finally when everyone was ready they got up, showered and got ready.

The dining room served a special Christmas Eve brunch which everyone enjoyed. The four Dark Ones were nowhere to be seen. They had disappeared at Christmas break and Tristan was sure they would not see them till after Christmas.

Trinity commented that it was nice to not have them around dragging down the mood. Christmas was a joyful time and the last few days would have not been possible with them around.

The day was filled with snow ball fights, hot chocolate by the fire, more Christmas movies and a ton of delicious food that was set up in the commons room for everyone to share.

As evening set in Trinity got antsy. Everyone planned on attending the Christmas Eve service at the cathedral, but Trinity did not know how she was going to get through it. She wanted to get right to the part where they confronted Cole.

As Trinity got ready she thought about how this had been a wonderful vacation. She had enjoyed every moment. She slipped into her dress and put her hair partly up. Then she realized she had a reason to keep her hair partly down tonight.

She looked at her high heels that she had bought for this dress and then looked at her combat boots. She glanced back and forth a few times indecisively. She grabbed the boots.

She smiled and she pulled them on: these are so "me".

She met her friends in the hallway. Nicholas looked at her boots. She smiled at him.

"Only you."

"Heels just didn't feel right."

"Nope."

"Think the Minister will care?"

"Nope."

"Think it's inappropriate for church?"

Logan chimed in from behind her, "Nothing is inappropriate for church, come as you are."

"Well, maybe showing up naked..." Trinity said.

Logan smiled.

"We would give you the shirt off their back and welcome you."

"So compared to being naked, boots is definitely appropriate," she said.

"Definitely."

"Good."

"Yup."

"Okay, let's go."

They all walked across the snow covered yard to the chapel, which was beautifully lit for Christmas. Inside, candles glowed and stained glass windows sparkled. It was magical and warm. Trinity knew tonight would be special, no matter what happened with Cole. This was the first year that Christmas meant more to her than gifts and Christmas carols. Tonight it was about something bigger than herself.

Logan and Trinity sat side by side in the pew taking in the music of choir that sang heavenly. When it was the audiences' turn to sing, Trinity sang out with all her heart. The words, "Joy to the World..." meant more to her than just words now that she understood the meaning behind them.

When they sang about the angels coming to the shepherds, she imagined a heavenly host of beautiful angels appearing. Knowing how beautiful they were, she thought about how overwhelming it would be to have so many attractive angels surrounding you. The amazing part about them is you are drawn to them. You are pulled to their inner spirit, not just their outward appearance. Trinity loved every moment of the service.

At the end of the program they sang one more song. As Trinity sang, "Fall on your knees, Oh hear the angel voices..." she began to cry. She closed her eyes, lifted her face to the sky and sang out. It was in this moment that she knew she was special. That she was here on this earth for something bigger than herself. She knew that even though she was just a high school student, she had a purpose. Life was bigger than just her, bigger than her experiences, bigger than even her universe. Life was big and multi-dimensional. The proof was in the angel standing by her side. In this moment Trinity was happy.

After the service, Trinity, Nicholas and the heavenly foursome hung around till everyone had emptied out. The chapel stayed lit and beautiful. It was Christmas Eve and the Pastor wanted everyone to know the church would be open all night.

Once the chapel was empty, the six of them gathered together at the front of the church. They held hands in a circle. Christmas music played gently in the background. The group stood together preparing themselves for their time with Cole.

Trinity prayed silently that Cole would be ready for what Tristan had to say. She was just recognizing what prayer was and how to use it. It was her power. Logan squeezed her hand assuring. She then remembered he could hear her when she prayed. She smiled.

The music swelled, the candles glowed and Trinity had never loved Christmas so much. Just as everyone was feeling the power of something bigger than themselves, the chapel doors slammed open.

The group opened their eyes startled, but ready. Cole's boots could be heard marching down the aisle. The sound echoed throughout the cathedral.

"What the hell is this?" Cole yelled out, flashing the letter.

"We want to talk," Tristan said, calmly.

"What? Is this some sort of intervention?" Cole asked, snidely.

Trinity could see that this was not going to go as she had hoped. Cole's heart was hard and he was angry. He hadn't come with an open mind to hear what they had to say.

Cole stood in front of everyone, poised and fierce.

Phoenix calmly said, "Cole, everything that is going on with Zoenn and his crew is dangerous and could change your life forever. The choices you make right now could send your life down two completely different paths. You need to think through each decision carefully."

Alaina chimed in, "Zoenn has you under his spell. He is poisoning your mind. Just spend some time away from him and his friends and you can think clearly."

"I am thinking clearly!" Cole yelled. He flung the letter into the realm of candles. Trinity watched it burn up with all the hope she had for this meeting.

"You guys leave me alone. I choose Zoenn. He helps me understand myself. He helps me feel powerful." Cole spat out at everyone.

Trinity tried to reach out to Cole.

"Cole," she said, softly. "They are hurting you."

For a moment Cole softened as he looked at her. Then in a flash it was over and his eyes hardened. They had a firm grasp on him and she hurt for him.

Cole pulled his hand away from her.

"Leave me alone," he muttered and stormed out of the church.

Trinity was confused. She had prayed that Cole would be ready. Where was her power?

"I don't understand," she said out loud.

"He's not ready and not strong enough," Alaina said.

"But I prayed that he would be ready," Trinity said.

Logan took her hand.

"Sometimes the answer isn't yes. Sometimes the answer is no, or not now."

"But I thought you were sent here to stop Cole from changing his life path," Trinity said.

"We were. But we can't force Cole to make the right choice."

"Free choice," she nodded understanding.

"So what's next?" Nicholas asked.

"Are we giving up?" she asked.

Logan smiled.

"Nope."

"This is just the beginning," Tristan offered.

"We are going to have to go to war," Phoenix said somberly.

"What does that mean?" Nicholas asked.

"At some point there is going to be a fight."

"Like yelling and screaming or guns and knives?" Nicholas questioned.

"Or teeth?" Trinity offered.

"Just prepare yourself."

"I'd like a gun if they are going to bring those sharp teeth to the fight," Trinity jested.

Logan smiled.

"A gun won't work against them. Remember you are waging war not against flesh and blood, but an immortal being."

"What about your sword?" she asked.

"It's not the kind of sword you buy at the mall," Logan said with a smirk.

Trinity grinned.

"Super power swords....nice!"

"We need to be prepared. Relax, we have some time. The fight won't be tonight or tomorrow," Tristan said.

"Tonight is Christmas Eve, the most special night of the year, let's enjoy ourselves."

Everyone grabbed hands and circled around, soaking up the candle light and the music. Tristan started in on a motivational speech while carol of the bells began to play in the background.

"We have to be strong. We have to be wise. We cannot let evil prevail. We will be victorious. We will protect multitudes of the human race from the evil that Zoenn and his followers are preparing. We are powerful. We are brilliant. We are warriors."

In that moment, Christmas was magical: the music, the candles, the snow falling outside the windows; Logan holding her hand.

Trinity was at peace, even though the earth may be going to hell next week.

Chapter Thirty-Five

Christmas morning dawned. Trinity woke up, washed her face but left her pajamas on. It was a tradition to open presents Christmas morning in your pajamas. Trinity ran to her brother's room and jumped on his bed.

"Wake up sleepy head!" she yelled as she bounced up and down.

"I'm awake. I'm awake." Nicholas groaned as he rolled over and grabbed Trinity's legs knocking her down.

The twins laughed. Trinity pummeled him with a pillow several times.

"Merry Christmas!"

"I surrender! If this is my Christmas presents I don't need one," Nicholas begged.

Trinity stopped the pummeling.

"This isn't your Christmas present, just a wake-up call."

"Well tell the front desk to cancel my wake-up call," he quipped.

"No-can-do. It's complimentary."

"Great," he whined.

The two of them got up and headed toward the commons room, arms linked. Christmas music could be heard. When they came in, the Christmas tree was lit up, the fireplace was crackling, the stockings hung from the hearth were full of goodies and treats. Logan, Tristan, Phoenix and Alaina were already there sipping hot cider and waiting for the twins.

Logan gave Trinity a gorgeous smile. He was almost giddy.

"You look like a five-year-old on Christmas morning," she observed.

"I don't get to celebrate Christmas like this very often. And I've never had someone to buy a gift for before."

"So you really are a five-year-old on Christmas morning."

He smiled.

The group came together and wished each other a Merry Christmas. They unhooked their stockings and began to open them. Trinity had stuffed her brother's stocking with a bunch of his favorite odds and ends. She had also stocked Logan's and the other's stockings.

She soaked up every second watching the angels open their stocking stuffers. The moment was priceless. They had probably never opened stocking stuffers before and every gift was exciting to them.

When they were done with their stockings they started on the gifts under the tree. They didn't just tear into them all together but took turns opening them as the others watched. There weren't a ton of gifts and the twins had more from their family than the angels so they opened a few at a time.

Close to the end Logan came over and placed a small trinket box in front of Trinity's face.

"For you. From me."

She smiled, took the box and carefully opened it. Inside was a white gold necklace. Trinity gasped. There were small angel wings attached to the chain.

"I love it," she whispered.

Trinity wanted to put it on, but she needed to give Logan his gift first.

She took his hands in hers. They sat facing one another on the floor. She almost didn't know how to start.

"I thought a long time about what to get. I didn't think you could really take anything with you and I wanted you to have something that would last longer than just your short time at the school."

She paused.

"You are special. This....this thing between us....is special. So...I did something...special."

Having said that she turned around and lifted her raven black unruly hair up. On the back of her neck was a tattoo of angel wings.

"Is that real?" he asked, amazed.

She turned back to him scrunching up her nose unsure as she nodded her head yes.

"I never want to forget this time of my life. I never want to forget you," she said nervous.

He cupped her chin in his hand.

"That's amazing," he whispered. "I am flattered. Thank you."

She grinned.

Her brother came over to see her tattoo.

"Impressive," he said.

"I had it done when we were in London," she offered.

"It's a beautiful gesture," Alaina told her.

"Mom might kill you," Nicholas said with a wry grin.

"Not because you got a tattoo, but because you didn't wait till you were 18," he added.

Trinity chuckled.

"Your parents okay with tattoos?" Tristan asked.

The twins smiled.

"They have tattoos," they said together.

"They just wanted us to wait till we were 18 before we started marking ourselves up," Trinity said with a smile.

Nicholas shrugged.

"I think you'll be fine. It's just too bad you can't tell them what the tattoo means."

"You never know," Logan said.

Everyone spent the rest of the afternoon snuggled up on the couch watching Christmas movies and munching on yummies.

Everyone opted to eat dinner in the commons room instead of in the dining hall. Just before dinner Trinity cuddled up at the window seat and looked out over the white landscape. Snow slowly floated down covering any snow tracks. The school grounds looked perfect covered in soft violet light. The fire crackled in the background and Judy Garland was singing, "Have Yourself a Merry Christmas" from the television.

Trinity didn't want this moment to end. She was full of warm fuzzies. It was a magical day. Her brother sat next to her, took her hand in his.

"Pretty perfect Christmas, huh?"

She smiled at her brother.

"What would have been perfect would be if mom and dad were here and we were able to tell them about these guys," she said nodding over her shoulder at Logan sitting across the room.

"I know," he said understanding.

"But other than that, yes, it was an amazing Christmas."

"Happy?"

"Happy."

Chapter Thirty-Six

Here she was again, up to her knees in the snow in a corset dress and her boots. The birch tree grove was to her right and she knew the small village was to her left. This time she was going to head straight. She needed to explore all her options in her dream before it actually happened.

She started to move forward. She pulled her cape around her, put the hood over her head and tromped through the cold snow. As she waded through the white fluff, she prayed.

She figured if she started now, then maybe Logan would get to her sooner than later. A blizzard of snow flurried around her. She tucked her head down and kept moving forward. If she stopped she did not know if Roan would find her and kill her or if the snow would simply freeze her to death. Neither option was appealing.

222

Once again she found herself trudging uphill.

"Step. Breath. Step. Breath." She kept telling herself. "Don't stop moving."

She came to the crest of the hill and she could see an old castle. She headed toward it. She carefully crossed the wooden bridge to the large antique doors. The door-knocker was ornate. She pulled on the iron knocker and rapped on the door. Silence. The only thing she heard was the wind and snow whipping around her. Again she knocked. Nothing.

She pushed the door open. It creaked like in a scary movie. As she stepped inside the castle she noticed the medieval decor. There were stone floors and walls. The halls were lit with fire lanterns. It was as if no one had updated the castle throughout the years. It was a step back into medieval times.

"Hello?" she called out. Inside she prayed, "Please send help."

She walked down one of the stone halls, brushing her hands over the ornate tapestries hanging on the walls. She called out again.

"Hello?"

No answer.

She figured it was abandoned as the village had been. She also knew Roan was going to show up at any moment. Instead of running up and down the halls panicking, she took it slow. She explored the halls, entered one of the rooms and looked around.

She walked over to the large two-story window and looked out over the moor. The sun had set and it was dark. She could see that the exterior of the castle was lit by lanterns and candles. No modern lighting could be seen anywhere.

She looked back around the room. It was a parlor of some sort. She left the room and explored down another hall. She kept her hand running along the wall to keep her bearings. It was very dark and the torches were spaced far apart.

At the end of the hall, there was a spiral stone staircase. She slowly walked down the stairs.

"Please send help."

At the bottom of the staircase was what appeared to be a dungeon. Trinity was a little worried. This seemed like a dead end. But she walked around exploring the different cells. There was straw strewn around on the floor. There were shackles hanging from the walls.

Through one of the iron-barred windows Trinity could see the moon shining outside.

"Trinity."

She heard her name whispered.

Fear left her breathless. She knew he was here.

"Help me. Please send help. I don't want to die," she prayed, quietly.

Trinity slowly headed back toward the spiral staircase. She ran her hand along the iron bars of one of the cells.

Suddenly, a hand wrapped around hers, her hand pinned around one of the iron rods. She turned. She was facing Roan through the bars.

"We meet again," he whispered seductively.

She stared back at him grabbing a bar with her other hand. He slid his arm through the bars and pulled her close to him. They were face to face, inches apart.

He inhaled deeply.

"You smell like freshly fallen snow," he cooed, "and lavender."

She was silent.

"Nothing to say?" he asked, amused.

 Silence.

"I think you know by now that you and I are going to meet like this in real life," he said, and licked his lips.

She could see the lust in his eyes as the light from the torches flickered.

"The question I am sure you are asking yourself is, when and where?"

Silence.

He let out a slow sigh.

"You make me want to be a better man," he crooned.

Silence. Then he burst out laughing.

"I'm just teasing you."

Trinity simply raised her eyebrows not amused.

"Nothing? Really? Or are you just used to this routine? Maybe we should change things up a bit?"

"No teeth. So far so good," Trinity thought to herself. Just stall. Bide your time and pray!

"What did you have in mind?" she asked, not sure she wanted to know.

Slowly he moved out from behind the bars that separated them.

"We have this beautiful castle all to ourselves. There's several nice bedrooms upstairs…"

"Stop," Trinity interrupted.

He looked amused.

"Not interested."

He smiled wryly.

"You don't have to be interested. I can just take what I want," he threatened.

She stared at him.

"You don't believe me?" he asked.

"No. I believe you. You are physically bigger than me and could drag me up the stairs and….you know. But, it doesn't mean I'm not gonna go without a fight," Trinity stared at him defiantly.

He grinned from ear to ear.

"That's exactly what I want from you….a fight."

"Oh, you want a fight?" she mused. Inside she was praying faster and harder.

"Makes things interesting."

"Ya, but I don't feel like fighting today," she said, casually.

Roan grinned.

"I can't but help love you girl," he said smiling. "You are feisty. You are smart. You know just what to say and when."

Trinity stared. She did not know if this was a new tactic to throw her off her game. She just kept her eyes on his mouth. No fangs. No bites.

"You know, I kind of expected your boyfriend to show up by now."

"How do you know he's not here?" she asked innocently.

Roan's eyebrows furrowed.

"Was he being played?" he thought. He looked to his right and then his left.

Trinity shoved him against the wall, he lost his balance.

"Or maybe he gave me his sword," she offered.

Roan leaned in.

"Then where is it?"

"Maybe it's in my dress. It's a big dress."

"Are you flirting with me?" he asked pleased and confused.

"No."

He leaned in toward her wrapped his arms around her waist and held her tightly to his chest.

"T R I N I T Y," he whispered slowly.

"Is this where the teeth come out and you tear my head off?" she asked.

He leaned in close to her face, an inch from touching noses.

"You don't feel me?" he asked almost staring lustfully into her eyes.

"I feel your arms and your chest."

"It amazes me that I have no pull or leverage over you," he whispered.

"So you are fascinated that I am immune to your powers?" she asked, biding her time.

"You are the first," he said, and kissed her on the lips.

The kiss was firm, yet empty and cold. It disgusted her. She pulled away as far as she could with his arms still wrapped around her.

"Nothing?" he asked.

"Nothing," she said, coldly.

"That's too bad. You taste so good," he said, drooling. His mouth deformed, his teeth grew and Trinity cried out.

"Please help me!"

Roan laughed coldly and said in a voice that was raspy and animal like, "If He ain't heard you by now, He ain't gonna hear you."

"Who said He didn't hear her?" Logan said from the shadows.

Roan turned anxious. Logan stepped into the light. Roan threw Trinity to the side and turned all his attention toward Logan.

"Where's your sword?" Roan asked.

"In her dress," Logan joked.

Roan looked at Trinity confused. Logan used that moment to step forward and raise his sword to Roan's throat. Roan's eyes flashed with fear.

"Roan, I think it's time you leave," he said.

Roan looked relieved that Logan was not going to hack his head off. He did not waste a moment and disappeared.

Logan helped Trinity to her feet.

"You okay?" he asked, tenderly.

"One second later and you'd be carrying a corpse back to the school," she said.

"I'm here. You're safe," he assured her.

Maybe next time you could show up before the teeth come out. I don't think it's good for my heart to race that quickly," she teased.

"Faith, Trinity. Have faith."

Trinity woke up.

Chapter Thirty-Seven

New Year's Eve Trinity and Logan were sitting on a bench in the snow talking. It had been an amazing Christmas vacation. After tomorrow, school was back in session and life would go back to its routine. In some ways the predictability of the schedule was comforting. In other ways she dreaded it.

"How can Cole go from being a great kid one day, then the next he's hanging out with demons, white-washing kids' faces with snow, and acting cruel and rebellious?" Trinity asked quietly. "I don't understand. This is Cole Hopkins we are talking about. California surfer boy, Captain of the rugby team, happy-go-lucky, the guy that liked everyone and everyone liked."

Logan sighed.

"Evil can be alluring. You let one bad thought into your head and those guys can twist it and help it to grow until you don't know who you've become. It doesn't take long for evil to sprout and grow."

"One bad or rebellious thought breeds another?" she asked.

"Exactly. It's why it is important to keep our minds pure," said Logan. "If we let bad thoughts and rebellious attitudes remain in our head we will have changed before we even know what's happened."

"I can see how that would happen," said Trinity. "I've had times when I've been depressed and if I let myself travel down that dark road, a day later I've made up all sorts of untrue bad things in my head."

"Everyone has dark days," said Logan. "But it's how we respond to that darkness that can determine what our life will be. If we stay in the dark place, it can only lead to darker and more destructive thoughts and behavior. If we recognize our emotions, and look for positive answers, we can lift ourselves out and not let our lives spiral down out of control."

Trinity nodded.

"So that's what happened with Cole?" she asked.

Logan shrugged.

"You know that demons have power through touch. They can be there and you don't even know it. They aren't usually in human form."

"Ya, ya, invisible wicked forces.....just great," Trinity said.

That sat silently.

"How does someone come back from that path?" she asked.

"You can change your life path at any time," Logan said. "You can stop making bad choices and instantly start making good choices."

"Has anyone ever done that?" she asked.

"Sure. There are many men throughout history, even some that instantly went from the villain to the hero, all because they stopped making bad decisions, changed their life and started doing what was right," Logan explained.

"So Cole could instantly change?"

"Absolutely! Anything is possible."

The two of them sat quietly. Trinity was relieved. There was hope no matter what the situation. There was always hope.

The night was quiet. The dark violet sky was beautiful with snow gently falling down around them. There was a party going on in the dining hall. You could hear the muffled laughter and excitement at the park bench where they sat.

Trinity broke the silence.

"When you leave, will I ever see you again?" she asked, quietly.

She heard Logan exhale.

"I don't know," he said quietly.

"Once you leave here, you aren't ever coming back? So I guess that means I won't see you again."

"You may…later, much later," he offered.

"You mean after I die and go to heaven," she asked, sarcastically.

He grinned, looking deep into her eyes.

She bit her lower lip. She did not know how she was going to go the rest of her life without Logan.

The two spoke without words. They had a connection that was inexplicable. It was unique. It was special but Trinity knew in her heart even if their love lasted, their relationship could not.

"Happy New Years," Logan whispered.

Trinity looked away.

"I hope so."

Chapter Thirty-Eight

The New Year had been rung in and all the students were back on campus bustling about their school day. Everyone was sitting around the lunch table discussing Nicholas' swim meet this afternoon.

"You nervous?" Trinity asked her brother.

"Not really."

"You got this in the bag?"

"Yup."

"You're creating high expectations," she said.

"Yup."

"Well then, I expect you to win all your races."

"Yup."

"Cocky little twerp."

"Yup."

"Geez, you know any other words?"

"Yup."

Everyone laughed.

"I'm just glad Logan was kicked off the swim team," Nicholas joked.

"Why's that?" Alaina asked.

"How am I supposed to beat someone with super powers?" Nicholas asked.

"Super powers?" Logan chuckled.

"You probably could propel yourself with your wings or something."

"I could. But I would have given you a fair shot," Logan jested.

"When are the other schools going to be here?" Tristan asked.

"The schools arrive at two, but the meet starts at three. Make sure you arrive early to get good seats."

The group ran off to their next classes, except Nicholas who was excused to go warm up for the swim meet.

Everyone was excited. It was always thrilling when other schools bussed in new students on campus. Girls were excited to see new boys. Guys were excited to meet new girls. It was one big blind date.

Later Trinity, Logan and the others ran over to the aquatic center to get a good seat. They saw Nicholas and waved at him. He nodded, acknowledging their presence. He looked focused. Logan had won almost all his swim meets. He was one of the best. He was in line to receive a full scholarship to any college he wanted.

When the swim meet started, Nicholas dominated. He won his first three events, but still had one more to go.

When it was time, he stretched and moved to the edge of the pool. Trinity looked into the stands and saw Roan and glaring angrily and mischievously at Nicholas. She became worried. Something was not right.

"Where are Zoenn and Marquis?" she wondered. She mentioned to Logan that she thought something was wrong.

Logan began talking with Tristan and the others. They excused themselves and told Trinity they would investigate.

Trinity glanced at Roan, and caught him staring at her. He winked. Ivy looked at Trinity, her split tongue slivered in and out of her mouth like a snake. The two Dark Ones grinned. Actually, thought Trinity, it was more of a sneer.

The swimmers lined up and when the whistle blew they dove into the water. Trinity watched her brother power through the water clean and fast. Trinity was relieved. Then just as quickly, he slowed. He appeared to be laboring in the water.

She stood up. She did not know what was wrong. He was thrashing more than he was swimming and he had not come up for air. Trinity started praying.

"Please help him!"

Just then, there appeared to be another struggle in the water. Trinity could not tell what was going on. All that anyone could see was Nicholas trying to swim, but it looked like he was being dragged down. There appeared to be water thrashing around invisible enemies.

Trinity knew her brother was not alone in the water. She knew Zoenn or Marquis was in the pool, dragging him down, trying to drown him. She also knew there was an angel in the water fighting the demons. Trinity kept praying over and over.

Finally, Nicholas seemed to be dragged to the side of the pool by an unseen force. His head popped up and his arms flung up over the side of the pool, his head out of water and gasping for air. Roan and Ivy got up and left the building. Whatever just happened, the struggle was over now.

Nicholas lay on his back gasping for air. The medics came over to examine him. Trinity ran down to her brother and threw her arms around him.

"Thank God you're okay. What was going on down there?" she whispered.

"War."

"You think the dem…" she started.

"We'll talk later." he interrupted.

Logan walked up and patted Nicholas on the back.

"You okay?" he asked.

"Ya. Sure. I'll be okay."

Trinity looked at Logan's shoes. They were soaking wet.

"Go for a swim?" she asked, grinning.

"Couldn't resist."

Chapter Thirty-Nine

Trinity, Nicholas and the angels were all bundled up in wool jackets and standing out in the birch trees. They needed privacy and this was a place they could always find it.

"We are about to go in battle, this could be too dangerous for any human," Tristan warned.

"I started this, I'm finishing it," Trinity said, stubbornly.

"This is not a physical fight but a spiritual and psychological one," said Logan.

"I know."

"The Dark ones will use their powers to harm you, maybe even kill you," Phoenix said, gravely.

"They...I don't know how to explain this to you, they won't be human when we fight," Tristan tried to explain.

"I know. I've had dreams," Trinity said.

All the angels looked at her at the same time.

"Are you still having those dreams?" Logan asked.

She nodded.

"Does Roan kill you each time?" he asked, concerned.

She smirked.

"Only the first dream."

Logan looked relieved.

"Does she have the gift?" Tristan asked Logan.

He shrugged.

"Gift?" Nicholas asked.

"Premonitions?" Trinity asked.

"Something like that," Logan offered.

"They aren't premonitions; the setting is different each time. If anything, it's symbolic of something that might come," she explained. "In any case, Roan doesn't stay completely human in my dreams. His face contorts; he has an entire mouth full of sharp fangs. He becomes animal like."

"It is a hundred times worse," Alaina said.

Trinity sighed.

"This is my course. This is what I am meant to do. I have been lead down this path and I am going to follow it. You talk about life paths. Well, this is mine. I'm in."

"Me too," Nicholas chimed in.

The angels looked at one another, silently communicating.

"All right," Tristan concluded. "We will keep you posted."

Trinity and Nicholas nodded. That was their cue and they left the group. The immortals stayed to plan.

On the way back to the dorms, Nicholas looked over at his sister and said a small prayer. He knew that she was more in the center of all this than he was. She needed protection. A guardian angel, someone to watch over her. From the birch trees, Logan watched as the twins walked off in the distance. He heard Nicholas' prayer, and he prayed too.

"Grant me the strength, wisdom and ability to protect her...and maybe send me a backup."

Chapter Forty

"Can I take the blindfold off now?" Trinity asked Logan.

"Nope, we are almost there," he said with a smile. He had a special surprise planned for her. It was a new moon and the night sky was indigo. The moon never looked so big and beautiful, but maybe that was just because of how he felt about her.

Logan planned a romantic dinner in the castle ruins near the school grounds. They climbed several sets of stairs to the rooftop, which looked out over the moors below.

Once they reached the top he took the blindfold off her eyes. She saw candles all around the roof, a beautiful table set for two and the stars twinkling overhead. It was breathtaking.

"It's amazing," she said looking at him.

He smiled. She looked ravishing in her red silk dress as it whipped around in the evening breeze. Her long raven hair flowed around her shoulders, framing her face. Her crystal blue eyes pierced the darkness.

He pulled a chair out for her. They sat down and the two of them began their dinner. Something had been on Trinity's mind and she was not sure if this was the time to talk with Logan about it. Her questions were deeply theological and she did not want to ruin the romantic setting. But Logan sensed something was on her mind.

"What is it?"

"What's what?" she asked.

"You have something on your mind. I can tell."

"Or you can read my thoughts."

"If I could read your thoughts then I would know what it was, now wouldn't I?" he argued.

"Good point."

"I was wondering how man can choose evil or want to do evil. I think if most people saw what I have seen these past few months, they would realize that evil is not something to be toyed with."

"Almost no human will ever see what you have. Most don't believe in anything bigger than themselves. They are focused only on themselves, and selfishness leads them down a slippery slope."

Trinity thought about it.

"The word 'faith' makes a lot more sense to me now. We just have to have faith."

"In what?" he asked, curious.

"In angels, in a Creator, in a world beyond our own," she whispered, in awe of all that was dawning on her.

"Why wouldn't anyone want to believe in all of this?" she asked with a smile. "Why not?"

"It changes the meaning of life," he offered.

"Gives it meaning," she answered. "Gives it hope."

She smiled. The revelations that were coming to her were a little like an "Ah ha" moment. She felt empowered.

"I am not alone in this world. Who wouldn't want to know and understand that?"

"I want to share something with you," Logan said, in a hushed voice.

Trinity was intrigued.

Logan gave Trinity a grin and took off his shirt. Large, beautiful, black wings appeared from his back. They were soft to the touch and stunning to the eyes.

Trinity gasped. She had never seen anything so magnificent. She walked around him and ran her hands over his wings, her fingers tracing lightly over the softness. When she came back to face him, she sighed, her hand resting on his chest.

"Thank you," she whispered.

He pulled her close and held her tight.

"You don't think I'm a freak?" he joked.

"Let your freak flag fly," she giggled.

"Ok," he said, and bolted into the air, still holding her close to him.

A shriek escaped her lips, her eyes wide. She was flying. They were flying.

They shot across the night sky until they reached a great height. Then they soared, Logan's black velvet wings strong and fluttering. She finally exhaled.

Trinity trusted him completely. She had her arms wrapped around him, but he held her even more firmly. Slowly she let her arms relax and fall back to her sides. She leaned her head back, arching her back away from Logan who still held her close. She floated as if she were in water. Her hair whipped in the air, her eyes were closed and a smile was on her face.

Logan dipped suddenly. Her eyes snapped opened and she grabbed ahold of Logan. He smiled.

"Hang on tight."

They shot downward until they were flying only a few feet over a meadow. Logan turned her around so she was facing the ground. She spread her arms wide and imagined that she looked like Peter Pan's Wendy flying through the air.

They flew across the field and did not see the little old man who was riding on his tractor back to his barn.

Trinity shrieked as Logan zoomed over the top of him.

"Blooming hell!" the old man cried out, and dove off his tractor.

"Oops," Logan said with a smile, as they sped off into the dark night.

"When he tells that story tomorrow, everyone is going to think he's nuts," Trinity said, with a grin.

Logan brought them back to the ruined castle where they had eaten dinner. He was about to put his shirt on when she stopped him. His tattoos and the dark wings made him the most beautiful thing she had ever seen. She ran her fingers along the feathers one last time.

"You're a beautiful freak," she whispered, with a grin.

He smiled.

"And you're freaky beautiful."

Chapter Forty-One

The next morning Trinity woke up and found a velvet black feather on her nightstand. She sighed, smiled and ran her fingers through the soft feather. Excited, she jumped out of bed, got ready, and ran to breakfast.

The dining hall was buzzing. Trinity found Logan.

"Thank you for the trinket," she whispered.

He smiled.

"Way better than a dozen roses," she teased.

Nicholas walked up.

"You heard about the ghost that was seen in old man Tucker's field last night?" he asked.

Trinity's eyes widened.

246

"Ghost?"

"Well, actually, old man Tucker says it was a red banshee."

"Uh oh," she said, chuckling.

"What am I missing?" Nicholas asked.

Trinity looked guiltily over at Logan and the two of them burst into laughter.

"What did the two of you do last night?" Nicholas asked. "And how come I have a suspicion the red dress you were wearing has something to do with this banshee?"

"Cuz maybe we went for a little....flight, last night," Logan offered, sheepishly.

Nicholas stared wide-eyed.

"You what?"

"What are you three talking about," Tristan asked.

"Nothing," Logan said, laughing.

Trinity gave her brother a "zip it" look.

Tristan looked from one person to the other.

"Logan please tell me you didn't," he said.

Logan smiled sheepishly.

"Okay, at least tell me you weren't the one in the red dress," he said, grinning.

"That I can do."

Tristan just shook his head and sat down.

All day the school buzzed with gossip of the red banshee. In one version, Trinity had sharp fang teeth and was threatening to kill old man Tucker. In the next, she was a beautiful angel in a long flowing red dress, granting old man Tucker a wish. She preferred the story without the sharp teeth.

Today was Chapel Day, most the student congregated in the stain glass windowed cathedral for a pep talk. The Dark Ones never came to Chapel Day. Trinity did not know if they could not enter the cathedral or they would not.

Today at chapel, Sabrina was all over Nicholas. She wanted to be by him and talk to him. She tried to cozy up to him. He practically had to peel her off of him. Unfortunately, Nicholas's girlfriend had gone home for a few weeks to visit her grandmother who was sick. Therefore Sabrina that she had a free pass to act however she wanted to.

When they sat down, Trinity made sure she was sitting on one side of her brother and Tristan was sitting on the other. The angels and the twins took up most of the pew, so Sabrina could not sit with them. Instead, she sat directly in front of them and kept turning around and making goopy eyes at Nicholas.

He point blank told her to leave him alone, but she refused.

When Nicholas came out of the chapel, Marquis was there waiting for him. Marquis was furious.

"Even though I'm not in chapel with you, I can see what is going on," he sneered. "Stay away from my girl!" he warned.

"If you can see what is going on, then you would know it was her that was coming onto me," Nicholas said, defensively. "I'm not interested in Sabrina in the slightest."

Marquis stared intently at Nicholas, standing inches from his face. The air was tense. For a split second, it was like Marquis human disguise began to melt away and Nicholas and Trinity saw his eyes turn red and teeth sharpen. But it was over before anyone else could see anything.

Zoenn had his hand on Marquis' arm and told him this was not the time or place.

"I will be watching you," Marquis sneered and walked away with the other Dark Ones.

"When he says he'll be watching me, does that mean he'll be keeping his eye on me like in the lunch room, or does it mean he'll be invisibly floating over my bed while I sleep?" Nicholas asked Tristan.

"You don't want to know," Tristan said.

Later that day the angels and the twins met in the birch tree forest for another pow-wow. The angels told the twins it was time to declare war. They were going to have to fight with the demons so that they would release Cole. He was not able to make decisions on his own while he was under their grasp. They were influencing him to choose evil over good.

"Let me talk with Cole one last time," Trinity begged. "I'll set up a time to talk to him in private at the Masquerade ball next week. If it doesn't work, then we go to war."

The angels looked at one another and decided it would not hurt to let her try.

"Saturday night is your deadline. If you can't convince him by the end of the Winters Eve Masquerade Ball, then we are taking matters into our own hands." Tristan told her.

She nodded.

Chapter Forty-Two

The night of the Winters Eve Masquerade Ball, Trinity was nervous and excited. The ball was always the highlight of the winter season at Shadowland Academy. Everyone dressed in formal gowns and costumes. Each person wore a mask. The costuming had gothic-steampunk overtones and everyone was dressed to the nines.

Trinity's dress was red and black striped. She had on a corseted top with a large bustle in the back and long taffeta skirt. As usual she wore her combat boots underneath with fishnet thigh high hose. She pinned her silver angel chain and trinket to her dress.

Her brother was in a shabby, chic tux with frayed edges. He had fingerless gloves on and a red and black striped cravat tie.

When the twins met up with the angels, they were all decked out as well. Tristan wore the funky oversized top hat that he had bought in London. Everyone looked smashing.

The well-dressed group entered the elaborately decorated dance hall. Students were dancing to the music. Logan and the other angels told the twins they would be back, they had some things to take care of. The twins went to the dance floor. Within a few minutes Dakota, in a royal blue ball gown and feather mask stole Nicholas away. When Trinity was alone a masked student swept Trinity into his arms to dance. He held her tightly with his strong arms.

Trinity knew just by his touch that it was Roan.

"Let me go," she whispered.

"You look ravishing," he leered.

"I don't like it when you say it," she said, angrily.

"Because you know I just might act on it," he sneered.

She shoved him away and ran through the crowd. She nearly ran into Logan.

"What's the rush?" he asked.

"Nothing, just a little dizzy and need some air."

He took her outside. She took a deep breath of the cool, winter air. It had started snowing again.

They sat in silence.

"I'm ready to go back in," she said.

"Good, because I am dying to dance with the most stunning girl here," he said, with a sheepish grin.

The two went into the Masquerade Ball. Logan took her into his arms. He felt safe and gentle, compared to Roan's firm and almost angry embrace.

Trinity relaxed and enjoyed their time together. She was still nervous about her talk with Cole later, but it could wait, this was too enchanted a moment to give up.

The Shadowland traditional masquerade song started to play. It was a fusion of rock and haunting opera. It was a choreographed, mixed partner dance, where everyone dances and as you go along, you switch partners. Trinity saw Roan out of the corner of her eye. She knew at some point she would be partnered with him and she groaned.

For the first few counts she danced with Logan, then everyone rotated and she was with someone else. Within a few seconds she had rotated again and she had lost where Logan was. She did not feel safe even though Logan was only a few steps away somewhere in the mass of students dancing.

Eventually, she was paired with Roan. He had his hands on her. She was pulled in tight to him. She did not like his grasp. There was anger and evil in the tension in his arms. They moved onto other partners and she was relieved. The music soared and once again she was partnered with Logan, it was a breath of fresh air, a relief, a reprieve. But as predicted she had to give him up again and once again found herself with Roan. Neither spoke, he just stared at her through his mask. She stared back. She went back and forth between Logan and Roan. At one point she was afraid he was going to steal her away out the door. By the end of the song she was exhausted from all the tension she had felt during the song.

On the last beat of the song, Roan leaned in and whispered, "I'll see you later," and disappeared.

"There you are," Logan said with a smile as he came up and gave her a hug. She needed it. She needed some joy. Roan sucked the life out of her. He sucked the happiness from her. She did not like being around him at all.

Logan brought back the laughter. The mood lightened. The aura around him was bright and he brought a smile back to her face.

They spent the evening dancing and Trinity was having so much fun she almost forgot that she had planned to meet Cole. It was like her Cinderella moment when the clock struck nine she froze and remembered her plan. She told Logan she needed to meet with Cole. Logan kissed her forehead and told her to be careful.

Trinity fastened her cape on and tromped through the snow to the garden house where Cole was waiting for her.

They stood without speaking.

"Thank you for meeting me," she said, quietly. "This is your moment Cole."

He listened.

"You have two paths ahead of you, each leading a different direction."

Silence.

"Those people are evil, Cole."

Silence.

253

"You know they are. I know deep down you still know what is right and what is wrong."

Pause.

"You've been my friend for years. I care."

She felt like she was not able to say what she needed to say. It was all coming out wrong. It was like talking to a brick wall. She took a step toward him and reached out.

"Cole, come with me. Leave them behind. Choose good."

Suddenly Roan stepped out from hiding.

"Why would he, when evil is so much fun."

Trinity gasped as the other demons stepped out of their hiding places. They all stood behind Cole.

"What is this?" she asked, fearful.

Zoenn smirked.

"This is your moment Cole," Ivy said in a whiny voice mocking Trinity.

"Those people are evil," Marquis also mocked her earlier speech.

Cole stood glassy eyed.

Trinity was saddened by his lack of response. She had high hopes that she would be able to drag him away from the clutches of the Dark Ones. She was wrong. Right now, she felt the need to run. Was this her moment? Was this her dream? She started praying. She needed help.

Trinity bolted out of the garden and ran as fast as she could for the Banquet hall where Logan and the others were waiting for her. As she ran, she prayed. She did not know if she was praying out loud or in her head, but she could hear her heart beating loud. Her black dress and red cape flew out behind her as she ran. She looked like little red riding hood fleeing across the snow. Within an instant the demons had caught up, grabbed her and dragged her into the cemetery.

Roan held her as Ivy, Zoann and Marquis hit her. Her lip split and she could taste blood. She prayed hard for help. She prayed for protection. The demons beat her as Roan held her. She did not know if she could stand up on her own, Roan held her tightly. Her stomach hurt, she wanted to crumple to the ground. She had not shed a tear yet. She still had faith. She knew Logan would be there to help her.

"Let me have her," Roan crooned to Zoenn.

"That's not our purpose," Zoenn stated.

"I don't care. I want her." Roan said licking his lips.

Trinity knew Logan could hear her prayers so she prayed "Don't let him touch me like that, please save me from Roan." She wanted Logan to know how serious this was. She knew he must be rushing to her.

"Fine! She is all yours," Zoenn said.

Roan threw her to the ground, pinned her arms above her head.

Suddenly Roan was lifted and thrown across the graveyard. Logan had pulled him off her and tossed him like he was a doll.

Nicholas ran to his sister's side and helped her up. She could stand and they needed to move away. A fight was going to happen.

Zoenn rushed at Tristan who threw a sharp punch and stopped Zoenn in his tracks. Within seconds there was a four-on-four fight. Both the angels and demons were fighting in human form. It was hand-to-hand combat.

Trinity did not know what she could do. Nicholas grabbed her hand and started to pull her away.

"What are you doing?" she asked.

"We have to help," he said.

"I know. But we can't fight like this," she said.

"No." he answered. "We have to help in the way that we can. We need our friends too. Let's go."

With that, he yanked on her hand and the two of them ran back to the banquet hall. They grabbed their friends, told them they needed their help. They did not understand, but they trusted the twins.

They all ran to the chapel. There were candles lit all around. Trinity, her brother and their friends got into a circle, held hands and started praying the prayer in the book that Trinity had found. It was a victory mantra of some sort that aided warrior angels in battle. Soon everyone understood the prayer and was chanting it together.

Spirits lifted and they knew they were making a difference.

Back at the cemetery, the angels and the demons felt the prayer and the fight took a different turn. The angels were empowered and took their natural form. Logan's black, velvet wings were visible, and he had a large sword which he yielded with ease. Alaina had beautiful wine colored wings. Phoenix dark gray wings that looked like they were so soft they would melt when you touched them. Tristan had brilliant crème wings that stood out in the dark night.

The demons outer human shell melted and you could see their grotesque demonic forms. They had contorted faces, smashed noses with large mouths, full of sharp fangs.

Ivy's skin took on a reptilian look to it. Her yellow eyes glowed in the dark and rounded. Her fork tongue slithered in and out of her mouth.

Each of their hands curled and became ugly ashen gray, wrinkly and triple jointed. Each demon took on an animalistic feature. They were ugly. Poison seeped from their fangs. Once again the battle started up between good and evil. But the fight became more vicious.

Back at the chapel the group continued to pray and chant. Trinity was desperate to know what was going on at the cemetery, but she did not dare leave.

When Logan was distracted in the fight, Roan slipped away and headed for the chapel. He wanted Trinity. She was his to conquer; he wanted to shut her up. He knew she and her friends were praying. He could feel the angel's strength in the battle.

Roan crawled up the side of the chapel like a spider and peered in from one of the stain class windows near the ceiling. He did not want to go in the church, but he knew he would have to, in order to stop the prayers and steal Trinity. He knew he needed the upper hand in the war back at the cemetery and taking Trinity was his ace-in-the-hole.

Roan smashed the stain glass window and fell into the chapel from the ceiling. The girls screamed out in terror unsure what was happening. Roan landed on his feet, his knees bent. He was morphing between demonic and human form. Trinity stood still. She did not know what she could do.

Roan grabbed Trinity while shoving her brother who tried to protect her. But he was no match for Roan's supernatural strength. Within a flash Roan had dragged Trinity off at lightning speed. Nicholas told the others to keep praying and to add into their prayer protection for Trinity. He ran after her. He could not just let Roan take her.

Back at the cemetery, Roan appeared with Trinity in his grasp. Logan stopped fighting.

"You want her?" he asked.

All the others stop fighting. Silence.

Roan had Trinity's neck exposed and his sharp teeth were poised to bite.

"She is going to die tonight unless you leave us be," Roan threatened.

Tristan looks at Logan.

"Roan, you know we can't let you have Cole," Tristan said.

"Then this precious little trinket is going to die," Roan sneered about to take a bite.

"Wait!" Logan yelled out. "Take me instead."

"Leave us alone!" Ivy sneers licking her lips.

"We can't leave you alone. You cannot have Cole," Phoenix insisted.

"If we let you have Cole millions will die. We cannot let that happen," Tristan yelled out.

"You want carnage? Then take me!" Logan offered, again.

"Not good enough!" Roan yelled and within an instant he threw Trinity to the ground, and sunk his poisonous teeth into her side.

Logan screamed out, "No!!!!"

He rushed toward Roan. Instantly the fight broke out again.

Nicholas arrived just in time to see his sister bitten by Roan. He rushed to her side, holding her head out of the snow.

Trinity lay in shock. She could not move. She was bleeding out her side. Nicholas wrapped his coat around her middle and tried to stop the bleeding. Meanwhile the war waged around them: angels fighting demons, all in plain view of the twins.

Nicholas cried out for his sister. He prayed that the angels would be victorious. Back at the chapel their group of friends steadily and faithfully kept crying out in their chant.

It was when Trinity through her pain whispered, "Give them victory," that the battle changed. The angels took the upper-hand and began to beat down the demons. Logan wounded Roan. Alaina demolished Ivy. The other ethereal ones defeated the Dark Ones. The four demons screamed out in pain.

"We relinquish Cole!"

They evaporated into thin air.

Cole who had been glossy eyed in the corner almost unaware of what was going on, dropped to the ground gasping for air. It was as if he had suddenly been able to breath.

259

Logan rushed over to Trinity, tears streaming down his face.

"I'm dying aren't I?" she whispered.

Nicholas, who was crying, endlessly kept shaking his head.

"You can't die. You just can't. It's not your time."

Trinity felt her life slipping away, darkness closing in. But she felt warm and safe.

The four angels circled around her. Logan placed his hand on her side where she was bleeding out into the white snow.

"Heal her!" he cried out, tears streaming down his face.

"Heal her," he whispered tenderly, leaning his face down to hers. Trinity's eyes were closed and she had lost too much blood. She was dying.

"I can't lose her," he sobbed quietly. "I love her...I love her."

Tristan brought all the angles together. They laid hands on Trinity's broken body. There magnificent wings covering her.

In a foreign dialect that Nicholas did not understand, he heard all four angels speaking. It sounded like melodic music. It was beautiful and for a moment he forgot his sister was dying. The sound of their voice knitted together and a faint silver light entered the atmosphere over Trinity. When they finished, they slowly backed away. Logan held Trinity in his arms in the snow.

Nicholas strained to see if she was breathing through his unabashed tears.

"What happened?" he asked, desperately. "What was that?"

A small breath escaped Trinity. Nicholas would not have seen it, except a slip of warm breath escaped her lips and materialized in the cold air. He collapsed down to her side and threw himself over her.

"Please Trinity, don't die."

Logan removed his hand from her wound and it was no longer there. Logan's hand was clean, no blood. Nicholas gasped. He looked at his coat that he had used to stop the bleeding and it was clean. Erased. Her wound had been healed, as if it had never happened.

Trinity slowly opened her eyes. She looked up at the four beautiful creatures; a small smile crept across her face.

"You all have freak flags," she said weakly, referring to their wings.

Nicholas burst out laughing and crying with relief at the same time.

"I was so scared," he whispered, relieved.

"You were just scared of what you were going to have to tell mom and dad," she joked, quietly, still lying on the ground in Logan's arms. She did not have the strength to stand yet.

"Is she going to be okay?" he asked, unbelieving.

"She is going to be fine," Tristan said, confidently.

Alaina went over and helped Cole up to his feet. He started crying and could not stop.

"Is it over?" Trinity asked.

"It's over," Logan whispered.

"Did we win?" she asked softly, loosing strength.

Logan smiled and nodded.

"The rest is up to Cole."

She smiled with her eyes closed. She was exhausted. But as she smiled, a tear slowly slid out of the corner of her eye and down her cheek. If it was over, then Logan would be leaving.

"Rest now," Logan whispered. "Just rest."

She fell asleep.

Chapter Forty-Three

Trinity woke up warm and comfortable. For a moment she could not remember what happened. But it all came back to her. When she opened her eyes she found herself in her own bed. She could not remember how she got here. She reached down to feel her side. Nothing. The wound was not there. Was it a dream? She did not know.

She sat up slowly. She pulled back the covers, her hand on her side, where the wound should have been. She walked over to the mirror and lifted up her shirt. She gasped. There was a tattoo of a black, velvet feather where her wound would have been. No scar, just a tattoo. A reminder of what had happened.

"Hey sis, up so soon," Nicholas asked as he bounced into her room. He was all smiles.

She lifted her shirt and showed him the tattoo. He looked surprised.

"Whoa, did you do that?" he asked.

She shook her head.

"It was just there."

He looked at her. She looked at him. They both knew what it was. The twins sat on the side of her bed. Nicholas put his arm around her shoulders and pulled her into him.

"I never want to lose you," he whispered.

She wrapped her arms around him.

"I never want to go."

"Deal."

They smiled. He held her for several minutes, soaking up the warmth of the hug.

Finally, Nicholas stood.

"Get dressed, we are holding court in the birch woods and you've been summoned," he teased.

She obeyed and the twins walked out to their meeting place with the angels. Cole was there.

Logan met Trinity, wrapped his arms around her and embraced her. He did not let go. Everyone stood watching. There was an undeniable connection between the two of them.

The group circled up. Cole took center stage.

"I wanted to apologize for the way I've been acting. I don't know what got into me. I don't know how to explain it, but I feel free now."

Cole explained that he did not want to have anything to do with Zoenn and the other Dark Ones.

"Is it too late for me to change?" he asked Tristan.

"It's never too late to change," he responded.

Cole was relieved.

"You were right Trinity, this is my moment. And I choose good."

She grinned.

"I'm glad."

"Thanks for not giving up on me," he said.

"You're my friend," she said, in a whispered voice.

He smiled.

"So, what now?" Cole asked.

"Focus on your education. Surround yourself with good friends. You'll find your way." Phoenix told him.

Cole nodded.

"For what it's worth, thanks again," Cole said. He turned to leave and then turned back towards the group.

"Why me?"

"What do you mean?" Logan asked.

"I'm just one boy. Why such a big fight over one insignificant person?"

"No one is insignificant," Tristan stated. "Everyone's life matters."

Cole nodded and walked away.

They could hear the school bell ring and knew they needed to get to class.

Trinity smiled and her brother put his arm around her shoulders.

They shared a grin.

"One hell of a winter...no pun intended?" Nicholas jested.

"Really?"

"Okay maybe just a little."

"You were a hell of a partner." Trinity offered.

"Really? You're going to go there?"

"Go where?" She grinned.

"Start with the all the hell puns."

"You started it."

"Ya...and like hell am I going to let you finish it."

The twins chuckled at their own silly jokes and strolled off into the snow.

"Nicholas, you are one hell of a brother," she signed.

Nicholas playfully pushed her into the snow.

"To hell with it!" she yelled as she jumped up and wrestled Nicholas to the ground, white washing him as the twins laughed and giggled.

Chapter Forty-Four

Trinity was in tears. Logan was trying to hold his back. The warrior angels were being called to another battle.

"You aren't supposed to leave me," she whispered. "This isn't right. Somehow our lives are entwined...forever."

"I don't know what to do," he moaned.

"How can a human and an angel fall for one another?" she whispered.

"It's like they say," Logan started. "A fish and bird may love, but where will they build a home?"

"Trinity sighed, then chuckled, "We need to find a lake with a tree in it."

Logan grinned.

"Will I ever see you again?" she asked.

"I don't know."

"How can I go on with my life? How can I ever fall again? You will always be there in my head, I don't think anyone can measure up," Trinity moaned.

"It's the wings, they make me taller," Logan teased.

She playfully swatted at him.

"You know what I mean. I've fallen for an angel...any human is just average," she said with a smile.

"You have to try to move on. Look back on this part of your life as a wonderful memory. A time that helped shape who you are and who you are going to be."

"And what about you?" she asked.

Logan grinned and looked down at his feet.

"Angels don't fall in love, remember," he said sheepishly.

Trinity looked at him confused.

"This is rare and odd event for me and I'm pretty sure it will never happen again."

Trinity looked relieved.

"You won't be distracted thinking about me?" she asked, partly joking.

"Severely."

"You can't. Someone else's life may suffer because of it," she insisted. "Whatever you do, do it whole heartily."

Logan smiled, wrapped his arms around Trinity and pulled her in close, pressing his cheek to the top of her head.

"You are amazing Trinity, and I will always remember you."

"And you Logan, are my snow angel, and I will never forget you."

Tristan interrupted their love fest.

"Logan it's time to go."

Logan looked deep into Trinity's eyes and whispered, "I believe in you."

Trinity smiled back, as a single tear slid down her cheek, "I believe in you, too."

For the last time he pressed his lips to hers, and time stood still. Her body was filled with warmth and love. She tingled from head to toe.

Logan released her and backed away slowly. Tristan, Phoenix, and Alaina began to trudge off into the snow. They headed toward the back of the birch forest, where they would disappear from this realm.

Logan raised his hand to wave and smiled. Then he turned and walked with the others.

Trinity smiled and whispered.

"Goodbye, my snow angel."

Chapter Forty-Five

Spring was on its way. The snow was melting and small clumps of green grass could be seen sprouting up. The cherry blossoms were beginning to bloom. Trinity sat in the bay window looking out over the school grounds. It had been a scary, and yet wonderful winter. She missed Logan terribly, but she knew she must move on with her life. There was no future with him and she had her entire life ahead of her. She could not spend her days and nights pining after him.

Nicholas came into the commons room.

"He sis, you have mail," he said, tossing her a letter.

Absent mindedly she tore it open, unfolded the note and read it. A small gasp escaped her lips.

"What's wrong?" her twin asked.

"He's coming back," she whispered looking out the window as if she were expecting to see someone.

"No. You don't mean…"

"Yes."

"How do you know?" he asked.

Trinity handed him the note.

The letter said one word, "Soon."

It was not signed; it simply had a black embossed feather below the single word.

As the reality set in, she stood and hugged her brother.

"I knew it, I just knew it," she said quietly.

"Anything's possible…he's an angel after all."

"My snow angel."

About the Author

Julie Bragonier Minnick, is an author of young adult novels. She loves to explore the spiritual, the strange and the paranormal.

Julie plays and coaches roller derby on the West Coast, which means she hits girls on skates...just for fun.

She loves to travel and has a pair of "adventure pants" which usually gets her into sticky situations abroad, yet those precarious moments make delicious stories. Readers will experience the places she has been and the adventures she has seen when they read her novels.

In her spare time, Julie watches way too much reality TV. That means she sits on the couch mocking the girls who cry when they get kicked off The Bachelor...when they've only known the guy for two hours. (Yes she admitted to watching The Bachelor.)

Julie is also a fan of video games. Okay, she's actually an obsessive gamer chick.

Julie loves hearing from young readers, so send her an email at Julie@JulieMinnick.com.

Go to JulieMinnick.com to like her Facebook page.